A HORSE CALLED

HERO

SAM ANGUS

FEIWEL AND FRIENDS

NEW YORK

For Clover

A FEIWEL AND FRIENDS BOOK
An Imprint of Macmillan

Feiwel and Friends books may be purchased for business or promotional use. For information on bulk purchases, please contact the Macmillan Corporate and Premium Sales Department at (800) 221-7945 x5442 or by e-mail at specialmarkets@macmillan.com.

Library of Congress Cataloging-in-Publication Data Available

ISBN: 978-1-250-04508-9 (hardcover) / 978-1-250-06213-0 (ebook)

Originally published in the UK by Macmillan Children's Books, a division of Macmillan Publishers Limited

Published in the United States by Feiwel and Friends, an imprint of Macmillan

Feiwel and Friends logo designed by Filomena Tuosto

First U.S. Edition: 2014

10 9 8 7 6 5 4 3 2 1

mackids.com

Courage is not simply one of the virtues, but the form of every virtue at its testing point.

C. S. Lewis, *The Screwtape Letters*

PART I

LONDON 1940

Chapter One

Wolfie stopped, distracted by the stacks of sandbags and newly dug trenches. Above Rotten Row, silver barrage balloons strained and sang on their cables. They were like sails in a high wind, he thought, or great prehistoric birds. Tolerant of her small and will-ful brother, Dodo waited, sighing loudly as Wolfie turned to look at some cavalry, dropping his gas mask to the ground. A team of grey horses was trotting brightly up the South Carriage Drive. Wolfie watched, transfixed; Captain had been a grey too. After the war Pa had ridden Captain along the North Ride for the Victory Parade of 1918, the medal on his chest, the cheering crowds, all captured in Ma's photograph on the mantel at home.

The horses drew closer and halted, luminous and magical as a troop of moons come down to earth. A frown creased Wolfie's brow. He remembered Pa, here in the park, after war broke out, the day before he'd left to fight again in France. He remembered how he'd turned, white-faced, from the animals he so loved, and said, "I hate all of it and what it stands for . . ." Wolfie had felt confused then, and shocked, and still felt confused now.

He gave a determined shrug, took Dodo's hand, and asked, for the hundredth time, his heart bright and staunch with pride, his face luminous with the spotless sweetness of the very young and very loved, "Pa did a great thing, didn't he, Dodo? That's why he got the medal. The bravest of the brave, isn't he?"

Dodo was silent.

"When the war finishes, Dodo, when Pa comes home, we'll start riding here again, won't we?"

"Wolfie, march," Dodo ordered testily.

"You look silly in a skirt, Dorothy."

This was currently Wolfie's favored riposte to an unwelcome instruction, guaranteed to annoy. Dodo scowled at the hateful name, at the hateful pleated skirt.

"And *you* have a silly name. Wolfgang is a German name."

Wolfie took no notice.

"He will be grey . . . with a dark mane . . . my horse will—"

"Quick march," Dodo instructed her one-man troop. Wolfie's world was filled with brigades and beating drums, banners and bugles. Only cavalry instructions would get the result that Dodo wanted. Wolfie gathered a set of imaginary reins, extended an imaginary lance, and galloped away, whispering to himself, "He will be brave and he will have a silver tip to his tail . . ."

Wolfie galloped all the way to the bus stop at Lancaster Gate. At the poster of the child and gas mask, his gallop faltered. Dodo waited, smiling.

"Take care of your gas mask," she chanted, dangling it before him as he turned, *"and your gas mask will take care of—"*

Wolfie snatched it and galloped on.

Stacks of dark green stretchers stood between the new brick-surface shelters at Lancaster Gate. A new sign read SHELTER THIS WAY. There was a shelter at school too, but it was like a damp brown igloo inside, with garish nasturtiums on the roof. London was in a state of perpetual preparation and precaution, something immense always on the brink of happening. Everywhere the endless warnings about gas masks, everywhere the constant instruction to leave London, to "give children a chance of greater safety and health," every day the announcement that the evacuation of children from the cities would continue. But how could you leave London when no one knew where your father was, when he might return at any minute, when you only had Spud to look after you, and she didn't seem to know any more than you did?

"We *won't* leave London, never, not till Pa comes home," Dodo whispered fiercely.

"Tens of Thousands Safely Home Already," the newspapers had said last week. Dodo shivered. There'd been so many photographs of the boats of Dunkirk, so many thousands of boats. Tens of thousands of returning men, the newspapers had said, but Pa still hadn't come. There'd been no letter, no telegram, nothing.

When they reached George's corner shop, Wolfie, thinking of his sweet ration, abandoned his rein and lance, and began to excavate a pocket, groping for the coin that must be there somewhere. Dodo, giving him as always her own ration slip, hustled him inside, with her studied attitude of tolerant exasperation.

George came out, waved to Dodo, then bent to chalk a message on the stand of the *Daily Mirror* to the right of the door:

PARIS SURRENDERS

Dodo's stomach lurched, her hands flew to her mouth, and she was screaming inwardly, *Where is he? Where is Pa?* Was he on his way back? Would he be back tonight? Tomorrow?

Wolfie emerged with two ounces of lurid Torpedoes in a paper bag, a violet one in his mouth, staining his lips.

"Have we won the war, Dodo?" he asked in a loud voice.

"They've taken Paris," she said quietly.

Wolfie had to decode the progress of the war only from Spud the housekeeper's grumblings and mumblings and his sister's occasional pronouncements. He frowned, digested this new clue, then dismissed it as not fitting with his view of the way things should go.

"Pa will get another medal, won't he, Dodo?" he said comfortably.

"Home," ordered Dodo, her heart thumping a drumbeat. *Where is he, where is he?*

She remembered the tears down Pa's face when a thin and trembly voice on the radio had announced that Britain was at war. When the National Anthem started, Pa had snapped the wireless off. Spud, roused and teary, the plate of roast beef in her hands, had said, "Think of all our men going . . ." And Pa had answered, "Spud, think of all the women in Germany saying the same thing."

Only Pa could call Mrs. Spence a name like Spud. Since Ma died, Spud had taken over the running of the house and the care of the children. She was so fond of Pa, so proud to work for him, that he could call her anything. But that evening she'd looked at Pa, shocked and perhaps a little wounded too.

Dodo marched Wolfie on. She remembered the OHMS letter recalling Pa to the Army, Pa's grief and his reluctance to leave the work he'd been doing, his papers and speeches about the conditions of the coal miners. He'd wanted, really wanted to continue that work. Then the second OHMS letter had come, warning Pa to report. Dodo remembered Spud saying darkly that Pa must either report or be arrested. In the end Pa *had* gone. Dodo turned into Addison Avenue. But now Paris had fallen; Pa must be coming back from France.

"Halt," she said as Wolfie reached the iron gate of Number 25, but her troop mutinied on the generous stone steps, was launching itself at the double door, erupting through it, scattering satchel and mask across the black-and-white-checkered floor.

Spud was standing on a chair in the dining room, her sturdy figure loosely enveloped in swathes of black sateen. "Ha," she said, fitting the last hook, hands on her cumbersome hips. "Not a chink of light will escape now." Dodo hovered beside her, a question on her lips but Spud dismounted, turned from her, and said, "Wolfgang Revel, must you always be such an explosion?" She gathered up his coat, cap, satchel, and mask. Wolfie ran to the map pinned above the sideboard.

"Where? *Where?*" he asked, his small hand hovering over Luxembourg and Belgium. "*Where* do I move our men?" Wolfie's confidence in victory had survived, undaunted, the flood of black pinheads into Poland, Norway, Luxembourg, Belgium, and the Netherlands. "Better off on our own," Spud had sniffed at the fall of Belgium, happy at such concrete evidence of the feebleness of foreigners.

"*Where?*" Wolfie asked again.

Spud put her finger on the French coast. "Twenty-one miles of water is all that separates us from the enemy. Just a bit of water and it's not just our soldiers that are coming back across that water, it's the war, coming here"—she jabbed a plump forefinger on Dover—"right back here." Spud favored a gaudy and sensational turn of phrase, and was prone to speaking in headlines.

"But have we won?" Wolfie asked, bewildered.

Spud shook her head.

"Then why're the soldiers coming back?"

Dodo, still hovering close to Spud, waiting for the right minute, asked finally, "Is it true? Are they—is Pa—will he . . . ?"

Spud pursed her lips and busied herself at the tea table with the plate of boiled beef. Dodo waited as Spud lamented the dangers of London, the closeness of the war, the suitability of countryside in general for children, digressing into her perpetual lament about the difficulty of knowing how to go about things when she never heard anything, when for all she knew anything could have happened and was she expected to go on forever alone?

Spud liked the children to remain aware at all times of the trying circumstances in which she had to operate. These were all familiar themes to Wolfie so he took no notice, but Dodo watched her closely.

Spud removed the remains of beef and served pudding. Wolfie stared at his bowl.

"Roly-poly with no jam is no fun."

He moved aside his bowl and emptied an old Highland shortbread tin onto the table. Lead cavalry figures spilt onto the mahogany surface.

"Will you play, Dodo?"

He picked up the horse he called Captain, after Pa's horse, and placed him upright, glancing as he did so at the photograph on the mantel of Pa on Captain, Captain's grey coat lustrous as a star against the dark crowds, the bronze cross on Pa's chest. Pa's medal for the Moreuil Wood, for the last great cavalry charge, was a flame to Wolfie, a flame to warm him, Pa's honor a light to live by.

Dodo glanced at Wolfie before turning to Spud and whispering, "Wasn't Pa on a boat—?"

Spud folded her arms. "I hear the Jameson twins have left town. And Posy Cayzer's going to an aunt in Wiltshire . . . the country's the sensible place for children." Spud looked emphatically at Ma's oil painting above the dresser, her largest canvas, of the russet and umber hills where she'd holidayed as a child.

"Are all our men coming home?" Dodo persisted. "Haven't you heard anything—?"

"Bath time," said Spud.

"It's not bath time," said Wolfie, looking suspicious because it was always suddenly bath time at awkward moments.

"How am I to know . . . ?" muttered Spud, collecting a basket of fresh towels from the laundry.

Chapter Two

There was no letter from Pa the following week either.

Spud was in a new sort of mood, a harrumphing, high-headed kind of one, rejuvenated by the fall of France, by Britain's "Great Aloneness." Posy's father had come back from Dunkirk on a boat. Posy lived next door and her father, Colonel Cayzer, served in the same regiment as Pa. When the Colonel came home, Posy had stopped visiting Dodo, then, shortly after, she and her sister went to the aunt in Wiltshire.

Wolfie lined his cavalry up along the tea table. "It's like this in Pa's barracks . . . one row on one side, and one on the other . . . Captain lives here, at the top . . . he has a special box with his name over it." Wolfie placed Captain so that he dominated the two files of bays. "I will be a cavalry officer with a fine grey charger. My charger will have hot bran mash and molasses like Captain and go on parades with brass bands and be clapped by crowds . . ."

"Drink your tea," said Spud.

"Wolfie eats derring and dash for starters," said Dodo. "Heroes and glory for pudding."

"You talk like a book," said Wolfie.

"The both of you, eat your tea. It's all peculiar words from the one of you, and horses-horses-horses from the other," said Spud, brushing aside the barracked figurines.

At dusk, when Spud began her elaborate blackout preparations, she began to mumble again about the proper place for children. Spud knew more than they did, Dodo was certain of that, or maybe just suspected something but wasn't telling what. The Cayzer housekeeper, Dora, was the purveyor of all gossip on Addison Avenue. Dora had probably told Spud something.

Dodo crept up to her, turning her back on Wolfie and asked again, "Have you heard *anything* . . . ?"

Spud paused, then set to again, adding, for the first time, adhesive tape to her blackout precautions.

"France has been invaded, Spud, so Pa—?"

"Bath time," Spud said, ready to hustle them up early to the nursery. When they were halfway up there was a knock at the hall door. Wolfie raced back down. Spud and Dodo waited on the stairs.

"Oh Lord," said Spud, taking Dodo's hand as they both glimpsed the young boy, blue-uniformed, the same height as Dodo, standing at the foot of the steps, holding on to a red bicycle with one hand, an envelope in the other, his eyes to the ground. Dodo stifled a scream and froze, suddenly detached from the world and dropping, the stomach taken out of her.

Wolfie grabbed the envelope. "From Pa. It'll be from Pa."

The telegram boy sped away, head down. Wolfie was tearing at the envelope but Spud stepped down and took it.

"Shall I?" she asked Dodo.

Dodo nodded. Everything was monochrome, remote and cold. Wolfie was reaching on tiptoe to the telegram, the front door still open. Spud folded it quickly and backed up to the stairs, sinking onto the lowest treads. Reaching out for Dodo's hand, she pulled her to her chest.

"Missing," croaked Spud. "Oh, Dodo, he's—your pa's missing . . ."

Dodo's legs quaked. Spud's words were distorted and swimming.

"What is it, what is it?" Wolfie was asking.

"He's missing, Wolfie, your pa's missing."

Wolfie looked from Spud to Dodo, the word "missing" forming silently on his lips, growing confusion coloring his face. Now he moved his head slowly and emphatically from side to side. Spud pulled him to her, but he squirmed away, still shaking his head.

"No," he said. "No. Pa wouldn't go missing."

"Oh, Wolfie . . . ," began Spud.

Despite the adhesive tape, the glimmer of moonlight on slate roofs between Spud's curtains was strangely bright. In bed, Dodo's body was rigid and frozen. The words "missing, missing, missing" drummed in her head. She heard Wolfie's soft, regular breathing. Asleep, finally, she thought. A dam broke and an unstoppable flood of tears burst from her.

Later, all tears spent, empty and hollowed out, she slipped out of bed and crept to the window. Luminous white fingers searched the night sky. Dodo watched, transfixed as a sleepwalker.

Missing, missing, missing.

Wolfie stirred, saw her silhouetted against the window. Clutching Captain, he crept to her and looked out. With interest he observed the searchlights and the large lemon moon rising over tall Victorian roofs.

"She hasn't blacked out the moon," he said, setting the lead figure on the sill where it shone like marble. He began to advance Captain from one end to the other. "Spud has forgotten to black out the moon." He looked up and saw that Dodo's cheeks were glistening and silvery, her eyes swollen. " 'Missing' just means they don't know where he is, doesn't it? But Pa can see that moon, he can see it too where he is."

Dodo saw Wolfie's fierce, starry eyes and her face contorted with agony and grief.

There was a knock at the front door. It opened and closed. Voices. The wireless in the kitchen was turned on. Dodo put a finger to her lips and turned from the window, listening. *Dora.* Dodo hesitated. Had Colonel Cayzer told Dora anything? Dodo crept to the door and beckoned. Wolfie crept earnestly behind her, glad to be on a reconnaissance mission with Dodo, though he knew that tonight this wasn't a game.

They huddled behind the kitchen door. Dodo, ear to the painted panel, frowned in concentration, heard whispering, then more distinctly, Dora's voice: "What're you going to do? The children can't stay here . . ."

There was silence from Spud, then Dora again: "The Colonel said . . ."

Dora's next words were an indecipherable, urgent hissing, then there was silence, then both of them were suddenly whispering at each other at the same time, their voices rising.

"That can't be true . . ."

". . . all back—that is, the ones that . . ."

"The Captain'd never do . . ."

"The Colonel says . . ."

"Are you sure . . . ?"

"You've got to face it . . . wouldn't dare show his face even if . . ."

When Spud spoke again, her voice was unusually meek. "I'll make the arrangements tomorrow . . ."

Dodo clenched Wolfie's hand.

The wireless was turned up for the 9 p.m. bulletin and they heard the reassuring growl of the Prime Minister, heard him say that Britain would "fight on, if necessary for years, if necessary alone."

Suddenly an air-raid siren sounded, abrupt and chilling. Dodo leaped up and pushed the door open. They burst in and threw themselves into Spud and Dora's ungainly heap under the kitchen table.

There was a roaring, another roaring, then a menacing screech, a second screech and a third, all at the same time—the air was bursting with roaring and screeching until Wolfie's teeth were rattling, his limbs shaking. He squeezed himself against Dodo. The shriek grew louder and louder like an approaching train. He felt Spud's shivering, the bulk of her wobbling like a jelly, the fabric of her skirt shivering like a sail against his bare feet. He scrunched his eyes tight, clenched his legs to his chest, but couldn't stop the image of a train rushing directly at him, straight at his head, couldn't stop the bomb that was coming straight at his stomach. One hand gripped a chair leg, the other a fistful of Dodo's flannel nightdress.

After what seemed a long while, the bomb fell far away, in a distant plop.

The single continuous note of the All Clear sounded. Spud recovered herself and began to disentangle her lower quarters from the table legs.

"Clapham," she said with satisfaction, then began to chide the children for not being in bed.

"That was the sound of human beings trying to kill other human beings," whispered Dodo almost silently. She had a good memory for words and that was something Pa had once said.

Dora was buttoning her coat. From the doorway she gave Spud a significant look.

"I told you, safer out of London . . ."

Dodo turned to Spud, mouth half open, but Spud intercepted her.

"Bed," she said abruptly.

Next morning, Spud steamed to and fro and up and downstairs with clothes and coats. When she paused for tea, she picked up two leaflets that had been slipped through the letter box onto the mat.

If the Invader comes, Spud read, *the order is Stay Put. Do not believe rumors. Keep watch. Do not give the Germans anything.* She put it down in disgust. Dodo sat silently at the window looking out. Spud picked up the second pamphlet and read: *Parents warned:*

Bomb Risk Near. Keep off the streets as much as possible.

This gave Spud greater satisfaction, which she denoted with a large harrumph. Loaded with fresh ballast, she picked up a basket and steered towards the laundry room.

"I've no choice," she said, her back turned. "Even your school's been closed."

She emerged, tank-like, with a basket of freshly ironed laundry. Wolfie pursued her into the nursery, where she was berthing, with the basket.

"But we can't," he said furiously, "not till Pa comes home."

"You'll be needing sensible clothes."

"We're not going."

"I'll take you on a special outing this afternoon."

"I don't want to go on a special outing," replied Wolfie.

Spud heaved a suitcase down from the top of a cupboard, and said, puffing, "We'll go to the Army and Navy stores."

"I don't want—"

"We'll go to Harrods."

Spud went back into the dining room. "Dorothy, it's all arranged. You and Wolfie are to leave tomorrow."

Dodo, still at the window, bent her head.

"But will I be with Dodo?" said Wolfie.

"You'll be together, they've said you won't be split up . . . it's ever so nice in the countryside."

Wolfie was struck by a sudden thought. "Will there be horses?"

"There are any number of horses, Wolfgang, in the countryside. You'll be going somewhere in the South West, you might even be somewhere close to where your ma used to holiday—those landscapes she painted." Spud gestured to the picture on the wall but Wolfie wasn't listening.

"There'll be horses," he told Dodo.

Dodo rose and drew close to Spud. "Will there be another letter . . . ? Will they . . . ?"

"I don't know anything—nothing more than you do."

"But what does that mean? . . . Where is he?" whispered Dodo, her cheeks streaming.

"I can't tell you any more than what you know already," Spud snapped.

It was a joyless excursion, Spud brusque and impatient, the toys in Harrods a dismal sight, the toy department empty of children. They surveyed a model trench scene of troops lined up for action in front of the Maginot Line.

"Why do we have to be on an outing?" asked Wolfie.

"Even the German soldiers sell well," an

unconvincing sales assistant was saying. Dodo turned away, but the assistant pursued her, holding out a uniformed doll.

Much later, holding hands, they groped along the pavement between shadowy figures. Motors with masked sidelights and blackened reflectors moved slowly along Knightsbridge. The headlamps of buses were cowled crescents of dim blue. Someone somewhere was intoning through a loud speaker, "Thou shalt not kill. Join the Pacifists."

A paper was thrust into Spud's hand.

"'Thou shalt not kill' is a commandment," said Wolfie.

"Love your enemies, bless them that curse you . . ."

"Disgusting, you Methodists and Pacifists and what have you," said Spud, jabbing her umbrella emphatically into the darkness. She never cared whether anyone listened to her and she was prone to underlining her opinions with an umbrella. Loudly berating pacifists and Methodists, Spud commandeered a taxicab, requesting "Holland Park" in a tone so emphatic as to imply disgust with Knightsbridge.

"Is God a passy-fist?" asked Wolfie, climbing in.

The cab glided over the bridge, the Serpentine beneath glittering like a stage.

"Twenty miles per hour regulation speed," said the jovial driver, "but what good's that if the dashboard lights are off and you can't see the speedometer?"

"How do you black out the river?" asked Wolfie, more thrilled by the glamor of a city lit by moonlight than the toy department at Harrods. Beside him, Dodo, looking out over the shining water, cried silently.

Chapter Three

"But why do I have to wear these trousers?" Wolfie grumbled as Spud hustled him into some prickly tweed, fussed over his buttons and collapsing socks. She plaited Dodo's hair and tied ribbons, which were surely not necessary for a train journey.

At breakfast she clattered round the breakfast table, setting down egg cups with a flourish.

"Have we got egg? Real egg?" Wolfie asked, amazed. Spud sniffed triumphantly.

"Can I have soldiers?" asked Wolfie.

Spud shelled Wolfie's egg, spread it onto buttered toast, and sliced it into soldiers. Wolfie beamed at the golden egg that wasn't powdered, at the butter, at Spud's tidy squadron on the china plate.

"There are horses," he told Dodo for the third time that morning, "in the countryside." He put the last soldier in his mouth, and added, "Pa likes boiled eggs too."

Dodo bent her head, fresh tears rolling down her cheeks. Wolfie went to the dresser for the shortbread tin and deliberately picked just one figure. Spud unpinned the map, rolled it, and put it in Wolfie's bag.

"Keep still, Wolfgang," she commanded, ready with a brown label and a pin. When her back was turned, Dodo rose silently, went to the mantel, picked up Pa's photograph, and slipped it into her bag.

They travelled to Paddington by taxicab.

"Can't get closer'n this," grumbled the driver, peering down the crowded street. He pulled up on Praed Street. "You'll 'ave to walk from here."

Wolfie was gawping at a long crocodile of children of all sizes, all with regulation brown rucksacks, with gas masks in cardboard boxes round their necks and brown-paper ration bags in their hands.

"You see?" said Spud, disembarking. "Everyone's going. Not just you." She took them by the hand and they joined the continuous stream of children and teachers that crossed the footbridge onto the main line platform.

"Barnstaple, Platform Five," she read from the announcement board, then forged a passage through the crowds of soldiers, children, and mothers to the gate. Soldiers and children swarmed along the platform. Row after row of seats were taken. Carriage after carriage was filled with forlorn, silent children.

"Why are the soldiers coming?" Wolfie's gas mask bumped his hip as he struggled to keep up with Spud's determined stride. A calm voice was issuing a series of admonitions over a loudspeaker:

"Hello, children. Please take your seats. The train leaves in a few minutes. Don't play with the doors and windows. Thank you."

Spud stopped and opened the door to the final compartment. She placed the suitcases in the corridor, beside a small tear-streaked girl clutching a yellow bucket and spade. "Sit on your cases," she said, slipping a chocolate Slam Bar, probably from her own ration, into each of their pockets, then whispering to Dodo, "Stay together. Don't let go. Don't let them separate you."

Dodo was silent. Spud was eager to send them away. Hurt burned like a fire in her swollen, glimmering eyes.

"Why are some mummies crying?" asked Wolfie.

"Because they can't go on holiday too," said Spud, disentangling Wolfie's hand from her own and placing him in the carriage.

Dodo allowed Spud a perfunctory hug, but averted her cheek from a kiss. She climbed in beside Wolfie and sat with her head bowed. Spud shut the door, her plump hand trembling on the metal bar as she pulled the window down.

The train pulled out, and there was Spud, running and panting, breathlessly waving a piece of paper in her one hand.

"Oh Lord!" said Dodo. "That's the paper with the name—with where we're going . . ."

PART II

NORTH DEVON

Chapter Four

After five minutes Wolfie asked, "Are we nearly there yet?"

After ten minutes, he unwrapped his Slam Bar.

"It's very far away," he said through a mouthful of chocolate.

"Are we at the seaside?" asked the girl with the yellow bucket. "*Where's* the seaside?"

A lady with a clipboard picked her way down the carriage, checking her list. She bent to talk to the girl with the yellow bucket, then turned to Dodo.

"Names?"

"Wolfgang and Dorothy Revel."

She scanned her list, tapping it with her pen as she moved from page to page. "You're not down here," she said eventually, examining Wolfie's label. "Who's looking after you?"

"Dodo is," said Wolfie comfortably. The lady looked at Dodo skeptically.

"We're on a private scheme," Dodo said, "we're going to be met at Dulverton."

The lady made a note and moved on.

"Spud's not very good at arrangements," Wolfie commented.

"Are we nearly there yet?" asked Wolfie later. He held Captain in a sticky fist, clutching him like a talisman, at the same time eyeing the pair of soldiers that lounged against the window, hemmed in by stacks of kitbags in the corner of the corridor. "Why is the war coming on the train?" he began, turning to Dodo, but seeing the sadness of her face, he took her hand and added, "There'll be horses, Dodo." Then, "They'll find Pa. Pa wouldn't go missing. Definitely."

It grew hot and fuggy. Morning turned to afternoon, as the train stopped and started, swayed and lurched westward.

In the early evening it shunted into a siding to allow a troop train past. Dodo heard, from the adjacent carriage, children cheering at the soldiers, saw soldiers waving their caps back.

"Does Spud know that it's a long way?" Wolfie asked.

Dodo shrugged and cleared a patch of the window. They peered out and saw a row of suburban terraced houses, their windows bombed out, patched with cardboard. Searchlights fingered the sky.

"We're on a mystery tour," Wolfie said to Captain, holding him up to the clear patch of window. "It's dark, there're no signs, and we don't know where we're going."

The gleam of a guardsman's lantern flashed along the corridor of the train. "Bristol, Bristol."

The door opened and a knot of pushing people swarmed up, servicemen hauling kitbags, civilians with suitcases. Luggage was jammed inside, piled high, the corridors now packed to the doors with soldiers and airmen. The door shut and the train swayed away.

Later Wolfie woke briefly and looked inside the food bag. Finding it empty except for an apple, he asked Dodo, "But is this for all of the war? Is this all we have till the end of it?"

Dodo ignored him.

"I want to go home," he said after five minutes.

"Dulverton, Dulverton. This train will shortly be arriving at Dulverton." The guard's torch flashed randomly as he forced his way along the train. Dodo peered out and saw a sullen station house, glimmering faintly through drizzle.

"Reveille," she said, shaking Wolfie. "Reveille." They clambered out, stumbling into soldiers and kitbags. Swarms of cold, tired children spilt onto the platform, squeezing into every corner. Drizzle shone in the dim beam of another torch. The train pulled away.

"Where're they going to put them all?" the

stationmaster with the torch wondered aloud to himself as he marshalled the tearful crew off the platform. Dodo and Wolfie wound their way through shadowy uniformed figures.

"This way, this way."

The Somerset accent was strange and thick. Dodo waited uncertainly.

"Can we go too?" asked Wolfie.

"I think someone'll come to get us," said Dodo.

"This way, this way. All on 'em. Get all on 'em this way."

Dodo didn't move.

"Yes, miss. You too. Off you go. Another train'll be here soon. Be quick if I were you—billeting officer'll be squeezing a quart into a pint pot with all you lot."

They were herded up a slanting street lined with squat houses of stern grey stone, then lined up around the four walls of what looked like a village hall. There was the sound of sobbing from most children as a nurse went round checking their heads.

"We're not supposed to be here," hissed Dodo.

A gaggle of women was ushered in, bobbing and clacking, pointing and picking out children. The lady with the clipboard was conferring with another clipboard.

"A girl. I just want one girl," one of them said.

Another was pointing. "I'll have that one, with the dark hair."

"Hold my hand, Wolfie, and don't let anybody take you away."

"I'll stand behind you, Dodo."

Wolfie "disappeared" himself, comically, behind her back.

As they waited, they heard the distant whistle and whoosh of a new train.

"Oh Lord," said the lady with the clipboard. "That's another lot of them." The women were still all talking at once, haggling like housewives over meat.

"Is anyone asking for a boy of eight?" whispered Wolfie.

"No. Of course not. They want girls."

Wolfie watched a girl being ushered into a car. "Will we get a car, Dodo? I want to go in a car."

The billeting officer led a woman towards Dodo. Dodo yanked Wolfie out. "We're together," she said quickly.

"Well, who's got room for two of you?" the woman said, turning her back. "No one'll take two of them."

"Not if he's not big enough for farm work," said another.

Again and again Dodo was picked.

"No," she said each time.

There were only a handful of children left.

"Can we go home now?" Wolfie whispered.

The second clipboard approached Dodo. "You'll have to be separated."

"No," said Dodo.

"Who are you? Name? You're not on the list. Revel—R, R, let me see . . . no, no, you're not on the list."

"Our housekeeper—Spud—made arrangements—someone'll come for us . . ."

"Who?"

"We—we don't know her name, we weren't given one."

"Well, we can't wait all night and I can't leave you here—never mind, we'll find somewhere. Mrs. Sprig? Mrs. Sprig?—Where is she?—We'll give you to Mrs. Sprig—Mrs. Sprig?—I hope you've got some proper warm clothes," she said with a doubtful look at their coats, then looked again at a woman who stood, empty-handed, near the door, tying her headscarf. Hairs strayed from an uncertain sort of bun at the back of her neck. When she turned, her face, set in a prepared attitude of distaste, quivered in surprise as she took in the smart tweed coats and Dodo's ribbons.

"Oh no, I'm not having two," said Mrs. Sprig. "No room."

"Now, Mrs. Sprig, 'three spare rooms' this list says."

The women conferred in whispers, Mrs. Sprig turning to look at the children from time to time, her eyes close set, her lips puckered, all her features contriving to be in perpetual motion, twitchy and undecided.

"Spud's arrangements are never good," whispered Wolfie.

There was more confabulation between the women, Mrs. Sprig relishing the attention, the commotion of the occasion, but reluctant to take a child home, let alone two.

"Well, I'll need the registration slips then," she said eventually. "That's what I need to get the government food and lodging money."

"I don't want to go with Mrs. Sprig," said Wolfie.

"She looks," Dodo whispered, "like a squirrel."

They drew closer together.

"Come along, come along. You can't stay here," said the lady with the clipboard, picking up their cases and depositing them by the door.

Mrs. Sprig turned to them and said, "I don't expect you've been to the countryside before?"

She paused, ready to enjoy the negative she expected. Dodo bridled and remained silent. Mrs. Sprig chuckled, pleased that the city children, though cleaner than she'd expected, might conform in other respects to her expectations.

"It's got horses," said Wolfie. "The countryside has horses."

Mrs. Sprig led them through the dark, to the back of the building where her pony and trap sat waiting.

"There's a blanket in the back. It's a bit of a way and the pony's old."

They climbed up and she tucked the blanket around them.

"I expect your father's away fighting, is he?"

Wolfie felt Dodo flinch, saw her turn her head. They said nothing.

"I hope you'll be tidy and quiet children," said Mrs. Sprig as they set off. "You're to start at school tomorrow, they say."

Wolfie turned to Dodo in horror and echoed, "School?"

They were both silent, neither having contemplated the possibility of school in the countryside.

"I have responsibilities to the church and the parish and I'm sure you'll want to respect my position in the community," continued Mrs. Sprig.

Again the children said nothing, huddling together, tired and cold.

They had no light of their own, but Mrs. Sprig's pony knew her way and they rumbled through the dark along an unmade road that curved tightly through a wooded valley, then climbed out onto an open moor. Through mizzle silvered by fleeting moonlight, they glimpsed the dark curves of distant hills outlined against the darker sky.

Occasional rifts in the cloud bathed the bare moor

in a ghostly light. Drizzle billowed like smoke drifts. Wind-bitten thorns grasped stubbornly at the bony hill.

They crossed the brow of a hill and the cart took a plunge, unexpected and steep. Below to the right huddled a coven of gnarled and twisted trees, blacker than the black sky. The trap slowed, Mrs. Sprig pulling hard on the rein, turning her head to them. A light flickered between the fragile, intricate branching. Wolfie clasped Dodo—she'd seen it too—they'd all seen it: amidst the gnarled joints and claws of the thorn trees, a beam, ghostly and floating as though not borne by any human hand. Again it flickered, and swam, fast as a phantom, uncovered perhaps by a coat caught in the wind, leaking light where it shouldn't, revealing a head of white hair, a white face strangely blotched on one side.

The light died. But that white face and white hair, the flickering beam, had left the moor stiller and stranger than before.

Mrs. Sprig turned back to the road. Clicking her tongue and whipping the pony on she was saying to herself, "Wild as a stoat, that one, wild as a stoat."

They dropped more steeply now, then took a turning through an arrangement of gates that had something to do with cattle. The track, sheltered by an overarching canopy, followed a tight, rising valley into a yard, the gate held loosely to its post with twine.

The yard, half mud, half cobbled, was formed on one side by a house that had, once upon a time, burrowed itself into the hillside, and clung there obstinately ever since.

"Dodo, can we go home tomorrow?" whispered Wolfie.

Chapter Five

Wolfie and Dodo crept downstairs to the big room at the back of the cottage. Mrs. Sprig was fussing about at the kitchen range. She hurried them to a huge scrubbed table and they sat quickly, sensing that she liked everything and everyone to be in their place at all times.

Wolfie stared at the huge open fireplace, the hearth oven set into it, the iron cooking pots on chimney hooks above. He thought if Spud were here, she'd be sniffing and harrumphing at everything. Mrs. Sprig placed two bowls on the table, each with a slice of bread in it. She took the milk jug and poured milk over the bread, then thick cream, from a second jug, over the top.

"What's that?" whispered Wolfie in alarm at such a dish, in amazement at the cream and milk.

"Sops," said Mrs. Sprig with pride.

Dodo wondered what Spud would think about so much fresh milk and cream in the countryside. They ate cautiously, then finding it delicious, ate on.

Outside there was a patter of unshod hoofs on cobble, and a greeting whinny from Mrs. Sprig's pony.

"That'll be Mary with the post," said Mrs. Sprig, folding a dishcloth, corner to corner. "Early with the mail today—she's probably got something from my Henry." Then she added to herself, "Or maybe wanting to get a look at the London children. Nosy old Mary."

Mary pushed open the door, placed a newspaper on the dairy slab by the door, and approached the table, surveying Dodo and Wolfie from a distance as though they were exhibits. She was large and shapeless, her eyes half buried by her cheeks. Dodo felt for the pony that carried Mary and her mailbag from house to house.

"I'm to collect mine next week," she said to Mrs. Sprig, her gimlet eyes continuing their minute inspection of the children. "One, I'm taking." She circumnavigated them as if to avoid contagion.

"School. Hurry or you'll be late," twittered Mrs. Sprig. "Hurry. End of the drive, right, up the hill and down the hill."

"School, Wolfie, get your coat." Relieved to escape the prying Mary, Dodo took their bowls to the sink and collected their coats from the door.

At the end of the lane, Wolfie looked up the hill and sighed, 'Why are the hills so big in the country?'

"We must write to Spud and tell her where we are," said Dodo.

A group of children—four of them—emerged onto the lane from a turning higher up.

"Let's follow them," said Dodo.

They hung back shyly, a few steps behind. At the top of the hill, the tallest, a boy, stopped and turned, the others then stopping and turning too, one after the other. Dodo and Wolfie hesitated, conscious of their soft London shoes, their soft London coats. They moved hesitantly on.

"Them're the Hollowcombe ones as came last night," said one of the girls, all of them staring as though Dodo and Wolfie were Zulus suddenly landed amidst them. "Them're everywhere, Mum says. Nowhere to put 'em all."

One by one they turned and walked on, caught up in their own affairs, as tribal and incurious as sheep hefted to a particular hill.

Wolfie reached for a small dark bauble in the hedgerow. "Blueberries," he said happily, a black stream down his chin. "There aren't any blueberries in Kensington Gardens."

"I'll write to Spud today and tell her where we are," said Dodo thoughtfully.

"Will she come and take us away?"

"No, she won't, but at least she'll know where to write to us."

* * *

"It's good we're all in the same classroom," said Wolfie on the way home.

There'd been other London children there, the single schoolroom crammed to the walls.

"No it's not. It's hopeless. Forty children in one class. How can I learn anything?"

"I like Miss Lamb, Dodo. The teacher is nice but I don't like sitting on the floor."

Dodo smiled at him. He was right, Miss Lamb *was* nice. The Causey girls had been nice too. They'd been on the lane in the morning. Chrissie was Dodo's age and she'd been friendly once they'd got to school.

Three days passed. Dodo hadn't yet received a reply to her letter to Spud.

"Hurry or you'll be late," said Mrs. Sprig at breakfast. Dodo toyed with her sops, not wanting to leave before Mary came with the post. There was a whinny from the yard and seconds later, Mary burst in, looking briefly at the children, then turning her head, her nose a fraction higher than before. Dodo leaped to her feet—Mary had a letter in her hand, and was putting the newspaper down, as usual, on the dairy slab. Mrs. Sprig was bobbing lightly on her toes, bird-like.

"Is that from Henry?" she asked. "Go on, Dorothy, put the kettle on for Mary, she'll be wanting a cup of tea I should think."

"No, nothing for you, Cousin Marigold."

Wolfie giggled. *Marigold!*

"Shh," hissed Dodo, then hesitated, stretching out a hand, hoping to be given the envelope. She saw Marigold Sprig's arms fall deflated to her sides, her face suddenly vulnerable and childlike. Mary was a little cruel to her cousin, thought Dodo, at the same time watching the envelope that Mary held proprietorially.

"This'll be for the London children," said Mary, turning the envelope over carefully, talking as though the children were not there. Mrs. Sprig sank weakly onto the edge of the settle. Dodo and Wolfie both stepped towards Mary, hands outstretched. She turned the envelope over once more, then held it out, midway between the two of them. "Wolfgang and Dorothy Revel, here's your letter."

She relinquished it. Dodo grabbed at it and started for the door. Mary turned back to Mrs. Sprig, talking still as though the children weren't there. "How do you *know*, Marigold, what you've got in your house, where they're from? With a name like that! *Wolfgang*. Think about it, Cousin Marigold, is it *safe*?"

Marigold's lips formed a thin O of inquiry, then quivered as she whispered,

"What do you mean, Mary?"

"Can I have it, can I have it?" Wolfie was jumping up and down. "Is someone coming to get us?"

"German," hissed Mary. "It's a German name. *Wolfgang*," Mary repeated meaningfully.

Dodo, reaching for her coat, froze, but Wolfie

retorted, "Wolfgang was Mother's father's name. From many-times-Great-Grampa."

Dodo grabbed two coats and hissed, "Shut up, Wolfie. Come on."

She dragged him to the door, throwing his coat over his shoulders. From the doorway, manhandled by his sister, but undaunted, Wolfie continued, "Many-times-Great-Grampa was the General of Quebec."

Mary sniffed. "No manners, them London children." She established herself comfortably on the settee by the fire and took a sip of her tea. "I've asked for a girl—I'm not being given anything like what you've been given. I need to know what sort they are."

Wolfie and Dodo ran out onto the lane and, at a comfortable distance from Mary and Marigold, threw themselves onto the bank. She held the envelope in trembling hands, turning it over and over.

"Hurry—hurry—open it," Wolfie was saying, but she'd paused at a distant tapping sound. Watching the lane warily, she could see nothing except the hedges shining in the silvery light. Beyond them, the primal hills, all ochre and russet. As they waited and listened, it grew to a drumming, a thunder, then a percussion of steel ringing on tarmac. The noise echoed and reverberated up the high-sided lane. They scrambled onto the bank, waited, trying to decipher it.

"Horses," said Wolfie, breath held. "It's horses."

The clattering grew and filled the air. They picked out the rasp of leather and jingling bridles. They squirmed higher, into a gap in the hedge, feeling as foolish in the still, silver morning as sheep stuck in a fence.

A torrent of huge, muscular hounds, all white-and-tan coats and pink tongues, surged down the lane. Then, behind them, horses appeared, heaving, coats glistening, breath steaming, clattering down at an easy canter. Wolfie caught his breath, transfixed by the splendor of it, by the weight of straining animal power, the flashes of scarlet, the bulk of bone and muscle.

"Morning . . . Morning . . . Morning," said each and every rider, touching a hand to his hat as he passed.

There was a shout from above: "Master on the left, Master on the left!"

The message was passed downhill from rider to rider, and the streaming, mud-splattered beasts were pulled over to the bank against which Dodo and Wolfie lay pressed.

Wolfie pointed to a rider in scarlet galloping down. "Quite good," he said grudgingly. "A dark muzzle, a silver tail . . . That grey is *quite* good . . ."

The rider caught sight of them there in the hedge, opposite the turning to Hollowcombe, and pulled up the handsome grey. Horses, live and tense, snorting and stamping, scrambled to avoid piling into one another behind the Master.

"Morning." The Master touched his hat. "Are you the London ones at Hollowcombe?"

Dodo nodded.

"Knacker's cart. Tell Mrs. Sprig it'll be there this afternoon." Touching his hat to them again, he spurred the grey on.

"That eye is not right. A good horse must have a big dark eye," said Wolfie. "Pa says so. Even a light horse must have a dark eye."

"*Knacker's* cart?" whispered Dodo.

Hot animal breath lingered in the air after the riders left and the lane cleared.

"What does he mean, 'knacker's cart'?" Dodo asked again, but she was bending over the envelope now. "From Spud," she said, biting her lip. Her hands shook a little as she opened it and read, scanning it quickly. She looked up and shrieked, "He's home! Wolfie—he's back—he's back—Pa's . . ."

She grabbed Wolfie, hugging him, the whole of her shaking with relief and release, tears in her eyes and on her cheeks.

"What does he say, Dodo?"

Wolfie snatched at the letter. Dodo snatched it back.

"Wait, Wolfie, I'll read it."

"Is he coming, Dodo, is he coming to get us?"

Dodo read:

Dear Dodo & Wolfie,

Your father's back. He's gone directly to his regiment. He'll write to you as soon as he can but wanted you to know immediately that he's here, and how very much he loves you.

I hope you are enjoying the country and that your new clothes are keeping you warm and dry. I am working in a factory making barrage balloons.

Spud

"Shall we not go to school?" asked Wolfie hopefully. "Perhaps we don't need to go to school here anymore . . . we can go back to London."

"Why does he have to go to his regiment?" wondered Dodo. She read the letter again. Spud's letter was full of holes, full of things unsaid, reserved and chilly. Dodo remembered her conversation with Dora. Something was wrong; Pa was alive, as Wolfie had always known he'd be, but something was wrong.

"I'll write to Pa and tell him to take us home," said Wolfie, fishing in his bag for a pencil. He found a piece of paper, and, eventually, a pencil stub.

Dear Pa,

I don't like Mrs. Sprig. I am glad you're back. Will they give you another medal? Please take us

home. Spud made us go to the country when we
didn't want to.

Love, Wolfie

Dodo folded both letters thoughtfully and put them
in her pocket.

Chapter Six

"Can we go to London?" Wolfie asked again that afternoon as they turned off the lane onto the Hollowcombe track.

"We can't go if Pa's still in his barracks."

"He'll get leave," said Wolfie. "You always get leave when you come home. And I don't really like Mrs. Prig."

"*Sprig*," said Dodo, setting off, trailing a hand along on a wire that was attached intermittently to wooden posts, all of them keeling like masts in a high sea. She stopped at a field gate, laying her forearms on it, resting her head, lost in thought about Pa.

"I want to see Pa," said Wolfie, joining her. He waited, his eyes close to the sodden wood, examining the surface of it, all a filigree of emerald moss and silver lichen. "Look, Dodo, it's all green and gold and silver, like a . . . like a . . . like something in church." He bent to study a damp and rotten stump, his eye caught by a strange sprouting of yellow and orange growths, weird as an elfin garden. After a while he looked up. "I just want to go home," he said.

"WOLFIE!" said Dodo. "We *can't* go to London. Spud isn't there. She's making balloons," she added, a little resentfully. "And she doesn't want us. Anyway, it's hopeless talking to you. Number one because you're a boy, and number two because you're only eight and for both of those reasons, there's no point—"

"I will be nine—"

"Your age will improve, slowly year on year, but for your being a boy there's no remedy . . ." She broke off and looked up at a rushing, whispering sound overhead. A dark, packed mass swooped low over the field gate with a mighty gusting, as if marking Wolfie and Dodo out for a premonition. It rose and widened and spread. A little spooked, Dodo caught Wolfie's hand, feeling again, as her thoughts turned to Pa, the shadow at the center of her joy that he was home.

"Starlings," said Wolfie as the torrent soared over the brow of the hill.

Dodo turned away from the gate to go, but stopped as she heard a new sound, the skitter and patter of unshod hoofs on the mud and stone track. A lanky figure, bareback on a stout pony, legs almost to the ground, was approaching, a sheep slung across the pony's neck.

"A sheep," said Wolfie, his voice wide with astonishment. "There's a sheep on it . . ."

The pony drew close and they both started, arch

as cats, as they saw the white hair, the red birthmark on the left cheek.

"That's him—it was him!" Wolfie said, putting a hand to his own left cheek.

Dodo scowled at him and he lowered it, embarrassed, as the pony came to a disorderly, snorting halt right beside them. Wolfie looked out sideways under truculent half-lowered lids at the violent red mark on the pale skin.

"You from Hollowcombe?"

They nodded, wary, in both their minds the flickering, phantom lamp on the moor.

"I'm Ned . . . Ned Jervis. From Thorne. You all right at Hollowcombe? Mrs. Sprig lookin' after you then?" His tone was friendly, his smile wide, brighteyed with amusement. "We'll be up this way with the knacker's cart later. Too wet, last week, couldn't get up there. Leave the top gate open."

"What's a knacker's cart?" Wolfie asked. And he knew Dodo was glad he'd asked because she didn't know either.

"For the old horse."

"Where's a horse?" asked Wolfie. "Where's a horse?"

"In top field. They left her behind, Bassetts did, just left her behind when they left Windwistle. Irish mare. Won't hunt again an'll 'ave to shoot her for the hounds."

"Savages," said Dodo, raising her head slowly, now looking him square in the eyes in disgust.

"Where's the top field?" asked Wolfie.

"Savages," repeated Dodo.

Hurt, and taken aback, Ned turned to Wolfie and said, "Follow the lane. Through the yard at Windwistle. Out along beech hedge line. First gate!" he called. "Leave it open for's!"

He banged his legs and the sturdy animal spurted wildly forward. Ned cantered off, one arm out, pointing left.

"I'm going to find the horse," Wolfie said.

He set off running in the direction of Ned's pointing arm. Dodo walked slowly after him, following the track as it curved and dropped, the hedges on either side rising from banks of stone cushioned with emerald moss. The dropping sun shone fire-gold through the vaulting luminous russet leaves. The lane turned a corner and Dodo saw a cottage, so ancient and golden that it seemed to smile at her as if out of a storybook.

"'Windwistle,'" she read, on white letters carved in a slate set into the bank. Two stone walls, a cowshed along one side, the house along another, together enclosed a yard in the corner of which stood an old apple tree, thickly hung with baubles of red fruit.

"No one lives here," breathed Dodo.

Wolfie was far ahead, shouting, "I'm going to find the horse!"

"Windwistle," whispered Dodo.

Wolfie was at a gate set into one of the yard walls, lifting the latch, following a line of oaks. Dodo lingered in the mossy yard, caught up in the mystery and magic of the abandoned house.

Wolfie ran along a line of trees, cobweb trails of ghostly grey-green bearding each silvery limb. He thought again of the horse—abandoned and alone, just left behind. He started running again—the knacker's cart would be coming. His heart drummed and he ran faster. *An old mare.* Geldings were better. He knew that because Pa always had geldings. Still, he pushed that thought aside and ran on, stumbling where the trees' licheny arms curtsied to the mossy ground.

Wolfie reached a break in the line of trees where a hedge had once been, then a second gate, but this one was splintered, punched in its middle, as if some angry beast had charged it in a rage. Had she gone? Had the mare gone?

Beyond lay a rougher piece of ground, in the center of which a ring of trees, thorns of some kind perhaps, formed a shelter.

There was no horse.

He cast around, looked behind—perhaps the mare had burst through that gate and escaped—but there'd been no horse in the first field either. Wolfie looked ahead again. "There," he said to himself, "there in the trees, she'd be in the trees, that's where I'd be if I were a horse in this field." He could see nothing. A sharp, warning *kuk-kuk* held him to the spot. There was a sudden clattering and a black shape swooped down. A second dark thing rose from the shadow and the two fought, midair, like raggedy witches, the first seeing the other off with an evil screech.

Wolfie moved on towards the ring of thorns. The outcast bird was settling on a branch, hideous and hunched, a sulking, hooded thing, black on a black branch against the darkening sky.

Unnerved by the ravens, Wolfie waited, watchful and wary. Where the trees shadowed the ground on the other side of the circle, deep in the shadow there . . . Had something moved? He shifted. Leaves rustled, twigs cracked underfoot, startling as fireworks.

He took a step forward. There, where there was a mound, part of an old hedgerow perhaps . . . what was there? He peered ahead but there was only silence and stillness. His shoulders sank. There was no horse, the gate was broken, the mare long gone.

Now there was a croaking, a *kark-kark*, then an answering *kuk-kuk*, a whirring from the mound, two ravens sparring, their muscular barks raised in sharp argument. Wolfie started, suddenly sure there *was* something—not just the birds . . .

The ravens sparred and *karked*, and spread their menacing cloaks. Another, more cunning than the others, waiting blackly on a branch, suddenly rose and swooped. There was more quarrelling, more clashing, flapping, and Wolfie sprang forward—racing—the shadow was moving—beneath the ravens—something was there and it was moving. He heard a whinny, wild and raw, a shrill arpeggio of pure terror—and Wolfie burst into a run, stumbling in the troughs where the fallen leaves were deep, shouting and flapping his arms.

He stopped, and stood, trembling, openmouthed, unbelieving, head swimming.

There beneath the filigree branches that spread like charcoal etchings against the sky, there in the amber light of a dipping autumn sun, a young foal was rising to his feet, improbable and exquisite, a head luminous and white, a dark tail, short and thick as a brush, wavering spindle legs, uncertain and tippy-toed, the narrow body and dark, startled eyes.

Wolfie caught his breath with wonder, his full eight years of dreaming and longing finding their rest in those dark eyes.

"My horse," he whispered.

The foal wheeled away, legs trembling, pausing, then lowered his head, bleated and nuzzled the mound. Wolfie's hands began to shake.

"His mother," he whispered. "His mother . . ."

He looked up to the ravens that waited, the hulks of them sleek and hooded on the black boughs, waiting blackly. One of them rose, clattering and squawking around the foal. The foal whinnied.

"He's scaring them off," Wolfie mouthed, his voice halfway between a whisper and a shriek. "When they come close it tries to . . ."

Wolfie drew closer. The foal lifted his head, nostrils

flaring, ears pivoting. He trotted, helter-skelter round his mother, limbs wayward, absurdly long and delicate. Wolfie saw the knife-edge ribs, the skin so fine and shivery that he was naked almost to the bone.

The foal nickered again and nuzzled the mound, lifted his head and uttered a terrified, heartrending whinny. Wolfie's eyes glistened. The foal stood still, his head drooping a little, seismic trembles wrinkling the skin like gusts of wind on water.

Wolfie moved a step closer. Head low, limbs juddery and weak, the foal watched him. Wolfie crouched and inched forward to the shadow on the ground.

He saw. He saw the eyes gone, the head picked clean, the clustering iridescent flies. The foal whinnied. Wolfie looked up at him. He saw the valor in his eyes, his confusion, as he clung to his dead mother.

Convulsed with horror, Wolfie yelped and leaped up, screaming. The foal whinnied again sharply.

"Dodo! Dodo!" Wolfie called desperately.

He was answered, from somewhere, by a different voice.

"Broke that gate, she did, got in here."

Another, answering voice, that Wolfie recognized: "Oop 'ere, oop'a the right."

Ned's voice.

"Gate's open, Sprig has'n' been oop here like as said she would. No one 'as."

A heavy, feathery horse had entered the field.

Behind it a cart bumped over the rough ground, in it two seated figures, one of them Ned Jervis.

"Over there. In th'ole pen p'raps."

Wolfie waved, screaming, "Over here—here!"

They jumped down and ran up and past Wolfie.

After a while, Ned looked up and said, "Nobody knowed she was in foal. Bassetts did'n' know, I reckon. Got 'erself in here out of the wind and died in the foaling."

The foal whimpered, legs tense, akimbo, dark almond eyes huge in the slender head.

"Looks sound."

"Hero. He's called Hero," said Wolfie suddenly.

The men spoke to each other as though Wolfie weren't there.

"'Ad twenty-four hours on her, I reckon, Drake, no more," said Ned.

"Don't stand much chance."

Hero nickered weakly and stumbled, crumpling to the ground.

"Get the gun, Ned, shoot the little 'un, an' after deal with the mare," Drake said.

Wolfie frowned, assembling their words like a sinister puzzle. He saw the man reach for the gun. Wolfie mouthed the words "knacker's cart," suddenly understanding, then leaped forward, eyes blazing. "No. No. He's mine. Don't touch him."

"It's one o' them London children," Ned said by way of explanation, "one o' the Hollowcombe ones."

"Did Sprig know she were in foal?" Drake asked Wolfie.

Wolfie shook his head.

"So she don't know then . . . She 'asn't even been up 'ere. Sprigs never liked the Bassetts, them or their animals."

"Shame. Nice-looking . . . ," Ned was saying.

"Don't stand no chance—probably didn't even get no milk off her." Drake was anxious to get on with the work, to get home, to end the day. He stomped over to the trap, picked up the gun, unsheathed, and cocked it. When he turned, Wolfie was standing between him and Hero.

"An' what'll you do with 'um?" Ned said to Wolfie, "'Tis 'ard to wean a foal."

"He's mine," repeated Wolfie.

"Get the boy away," said Drake.

"Let the lad have him, won't do no harm."

Drake lowered the gun. Ned was kneeling, inspecting the mare's belly. "'E nursed from her, 'e's got a chance," he said.

"Get the boy away then. Get the boy and it away."

Ned held a hand out. A minute or so passed. The foal whinnied and tossed its head, struggling to his forelegs. Ned kept his hand out. The foal paused, then lowered his head, raised it suddenly and swung it away, forelegs doubled, trembling, ready to rise. Ned waited. The foal inched his head back. Ned blew gently into the air but made no other movement. The foal jerked its head away, paused, then brought it slowly back round again. Still Ned was blowing, and now the head was reaching to him, nostrils quivering, and Ned was blowing softly onto the dark muzzle, one hand inching up the side of the neck.

"Hero . . . Hero . . . ," Wolfie whispered.

"Steady there." Ned was still blowing, still scratching, inching his hand higher. The grey head was drooping, eyes closing. Wolfie eyed again the strange figure of Ned Jervis, the whiteness of his hair, the redness of his cheek, saw how he now had one arm under the foal's neck, the other over his back. Ned was catching him up, rising, walking, beckoning with a jerk of his head for Wolfie to follow.

"See, 'e'll need a blanket and some honey."

As Ned walked, he gathered some skin on Hero's neck, pinching it together, then releasing it. A ridge of dappled skin remained, as if still held by Ned's fingers.

"Dehydrated. Needs water. An' milk."

Wolfie ran alongside, longing to touch, to hold.

"Ten pints of milk every twenty-four hours. Not cow's milk, mind."

Wolfie did not know of any other kind of milk. "Not cow's . . . ?"

Ned was smiling. "A lactatin' goat's what you'll be needing. Or sheep. Sheep're easier to come by roun' 'ere."

At the broken gate he said, "For tonight, two egg yolks, with water an' cod-liver oil. Keep 'im warm, see.

Same size as you today, bigger 'an you tomorrer. Grow as you watch 'em, they do. Feed him every half an hour. From a plate if you an't got a bottle."

"Dodo, Dodo!" Wolfie was calling, beside himself with longing for her to see. "Dodo, where are you?"

She was waiting in the yard at Windwistle, jumping up as she heard Wolfie, turning round-eyed with disbelief as Ned walked on past her, holding a very young grey foal, as though it were a large dog, saying, "Get a blanket."

Dodo eyed Ned warily. Wolfie was running ahead to the stable, shouting, "He's grey, Dodo and he's—he's—perfect." He unlatched the door, shoving it with his shoulder to force it open. Inside, old straw, dirtied by birds, covered the earth ground. A stack of old logs was piled high in one corner, rough kindling in another.

"I haven't got a blanket."

"Then your jumper, take it off. And you'll need tinned milk for tonight." Ned gathered together scattered straw with his feet. "Clean enough," he said, kicking it over and heaping it up. Wolfie hovered at his side. Ned crouched and laid Hero down.

"Scratch him on his neck, see, that's what she would have done. If you an't got a syringe, use your finger, but he'll be needing the honey."

"Honey. Egg. Water. Condensed milk," said Wolfie.

"Aye, an' cod-liver oil if you got it," said Ned, fluffing up the bedding.

"He's called Hero," whispered Wolfie to Dodo.

From the door Ned bid them good luck. He paused and looked up over his shoulder, listening. There was a throbbing and droning sound. "More load-shedding tonight," he said, grimacing. "On their way back—they've been bombing Bristol or Swansea." They looked at him, uncomprehending. "German bombers lighten their load over us on their way 'ome." Ned grinned. "Good luck with 'un."

Wolfie looked at Dodo. "There's honey in Mrs. Sprig's larder," he said.

Chapter Seven

Mrs. Sprig's door opened. Halfway down the stairs, Wolfie froze, shrinking against the oak panelling, heart thumping.

Dodo stepped into the dim light of the landing. "It's only me," she said, "going to fetch a glass of water."

"Fetch it then, and I'll wait." Mrs. Sprig hugged her bed jacket to herself, her face pinched with anxiety at the irregular and unpredictable movements of children.

"Yes." Dodo motioned with a hand behind her back for Wolfie to go, then walked on down the landing, heavily, to cover any noise he might make.

Clinging to the shadow, he crept down. In the boot room he picked up his coat, then the basket Dodo had prepared, a blanket placed carefully over the top.

Pressed against the wall of the porch, Wolfie considered the distance across the yard to the gate. He shrugged his coat on over his pajamas. If he kept to this side of the yard, kept to the wall of the house, he'd get to the gate without being seen. He waited for Dodo, peering out into the black and silver night, straining to hear any movement from the house. From inside he heard first one door shut, then the sound of a second.

"She's not coming," he whispered to himself.

He stretched out a hand behind him and pulled the door softly to, without latching it.

He tiptoed along two walls of the yard, then out through the gate. On the lane he broke into a run, pebbles clinging between bare toes, the ground already wet with dew. The way here was shrouded by trees, the darkness thickening where the track swung down over the stream. Wolfie stopped, unnerved, heart pounding, wishing Dodo were with him, hoping she'd come. He breathed deeply in, deeply out, to calm himself. *Hero*. Hero was up there, alone and hungry. Wolfie set off again at a run, the basket bumping against his side, only the twinkling of a tiny runnel giving him something to follow. The path began to climb. He looked up into the overarching trees. A spray of stars hung between the silvery branches, as though caught in a net.

"I'm coming, Hero, I'm coming, and I've got everything you need," Wolfie was whispering. "Honey, milk, egg."

He pushed open the door.

The slender grey body was sprawled on the straw. Hero made as if to rise, starting with fear, but sank down, tremulous and weak. Wolfie crouched beside him, spilling the basket in his hurry. He inched a hand towards the narrow, dappled neck.

"*Scratch, Wolfie, scratch their necks. That's what they do to each other. They don't like pats,*" Pa had said when he'd taken them to the stables of his barracks.

Wolfie ran his hand down a forearm, around the large bone of the knee, closing his hand, wonderingly, in a ring around the long cannon bone of a leg. He measured the length of his own arm against Hero's foreleg, then felt the surprising softness of a young hoof.

Then he scooped out a finger of honey and swirled it into the jar of water Dodo had prepared. He extended his hand and Hero's head turned, breathing heavily, nostrils flaring. Wolfie inched his palm closer and waited. Hero drew his head closer, nostrils wide and rosy pink. Wolfie's hand was still, his eyes watching as the velvet ears flickered.

Hero's head drew closer still, the dark almond eye watching, then closer still, and Wolfie felt the soft muzzle on his palm, felt the lips open and snuffle, snuffle again, finding the honey, then snorting and slurping. Wolfie poured more honey mixture and held out his palm, watching Hero as Hero watched him. Straightaway Hero snuffled and snorted again at his palm.

When there was no more water, Wolfie took a torch from the basket and poked around the walls of the building. Finally he found a feed scoop in a bucket by the door. He broke the egg onto it, then some condensed milk. Hero lifted his head, suspicious and wary, then inched it round slowly, nostrils twitching, and suddenly slurping at the strange new food, then snuffling and blowing and slurping and then nuzzling Wolfie for more, almost knocking the condensed milk can from his hand as he upended it over the scoop. Again Hero wet his snout and blew and slurped and sloshed, and Wolfie laughed with the sweetness of it.

Hero was tiring. Like a baby, Wolfie thought, seeing the eyelids droop, the long straight lashes dark against the pale furry coat. Wolfie placed his hand on Hero's narrow forehead. His lips were twitching. Dreaming of milk and honey, Wolfie thought to himself. His hand followed the crest of Hero's neck, down to the withers. He felt the muscles relax and soften under his stroking. He ran his hand down the shoulder, along the rib, and felt there, beneath his hand, the pulse of a heart beating.

He drew the blanket slowly over Hero, then lay down, there, beside his horse, in the quiet of night, in the prickle and smell of straw, the dark stable as peaceful as the calm of a church, the silence full as a prayer.

The cuffs of his pajamas sticky and sweet with milk, Wolfie grew warm and drowsy, edging closer to Hero. He laid his head on the straw, and watched

Hero's ears flicker and then, eventually, still, the eyelids half close. He grew conscious in the stillness of the beating of his own heart, and the rib cage beside him that rose and fell, rose and fell. Over the barn door hung a night more starry than he'd ever known.

Chapter Eight

When Dodo woke, it was too late. She yanked her shoes on and raced down the stairs. She'd wanted to get to Windwistle, to drag Wolfie back before Mrs. Sprig woke but she'd fallen into a deep sleep just before dawn.

Mrs. Sprig was downstairs, already busy. The fire was lit under the round-bottomed copper, Mrs. Sprig all a fever of washing and boiling. Dodo eyed the front door and hesitated.

"Where's Wolfgang? Tell him to hurry," called Mrs. Sprig's voice from a cloud of steaming and boiling laundry in the small room beyond the kitchen. Dodo glanced again at the door. It was flung open and Wolfie erupted into the room, straw in his hair, straw clinging to his pajamas. Mrs. Sprig stepped into the kitchen, a wet sheet in her arms, and looked at him, openmouthed.

"What's going on?" she demanded.

Wolfie avoided her and sat quickly on the bench at

the table. Dodo sat beside him and hurriedly picked out some straw from his hair.

"Can I ask . . . ?" began Mrs. Sprig.

But Wolfie could contain himself no longer. "Dodo! Dodo!" he burst out. "He ate it all, all of it . . ."

"Who ate what?"

"Hero—there's a—I've got a foal."

"Go and get dressed, Wolfie." Dodo was pushing him towards the stairs.

Still clutching her sheet to her bosom, Mrs. Sprig followed them to the foot of the stairs and watched him go up, her mouth hanging open. "Can't have this, just can't *have* all this . . . not knowing what's going on in my own house . . ."

Later that afternoon in the kitchen, after he'd visited Hero at Windwistle, Wolfie hissed, "He drank from a bucket, all of it, a whole bucket."

"What bucket?" whispered Dodo.

"I don't know—a whole bucket—but he drank all of it." Wolfie opened his arms wide to express the great quantity of milk consumed by Hero.

"But who gave you a bucket of milk?" hissed Dodo.

Wolfie lowered his eyes. "I don't know, but it was definitely for Hero, because it was left outside his stable."

"It must have been Ned," said Dodo.

Wolfie wondered what Spud would think about so much fresh milk being left outside horses' doors, then his head turned to the eggs that were accumulating in a basket by the larder door.

"My son, Henry, will be home on leave soon," said Mrs. Sprig, intercepting Wolfie's glance.

"Has Henry got a medal?" asked Wolfie.

"Shut up, Wolfie," said Dodo.

The eggs are for Henry, thought Wolfie resentfully. Mrs. Sprig was a squirrel, just like Dodo said. A squirrel with a very strong tendency to hoard.

Later, he perched on the bedroom with a postcard and a pencil. He'd chosen a print of a mounted huntsman, a bugle to his lips, a group of staghounds at his heel.

Dear Pa,

You must come here. I have a horse. He is grey. He has dark eyes. He has no mother so he has to drink condensed milk or goat's milk which is not very nice. There is a shop. It has pear drops. It is easy to buy eggs but they only had one tin of condensed milk and Hero has drunk it all. Please come soon. Please bring tins of milk. We are with Mrs. Sprig in Hollowcombe. She is not very nice to us.

Love, Wolfie

PS You must come very soon. He is called Hero after you, Pa. He likes honey too.

PPS I am in the same class as Dodo. I like the school here.

A week later, the letter that Dodo both longed for and feared was waiting for them on their return from school.

"Pa!" Wolfie shouted. "It's from Pa!" They took it up to Windwistle and read it together there on the straw, as Hero wandered around, exploring everything with his muzzle, nuzzling Wolfie for food.

" 'My darling children . . . ,' " Dodo read aloud:

I've missed you so very much.

Honey is very important for a young horse, Wolfie, especially if he didn't feed from his dam. A good grey will have a silver tip to his tail. Does Hero have that?

Dodo, do you have paints and brushes there? Shall I send you some? Ma used to holiday somewhere close to where you are. I'll look up the name of the house one day—Spud knows where Ma's papers are but she's away making barrage balloons somewhere. I don't think she enjoyed the bombs in London.

It may be a while before I see you—

Dodo's voice grew quiet and rushed. Wolfie listened, his eyes following Hero.

—but there is something I must tell you, something that will come as a shock to you both, but I know that I must tell you and that I must defend myself to you both.

I'm at my regiment's headquarters. I have handed myself in, and am being held here on suspicion of having committed an offense.

Dodo read on to herself, almost whispering.

I haven't been charged with this offense and hope that I won't be, though I will probably be questioned and have to go through a disciplinary procedure. Then, I think, I'll be free and able to see you both and perhaps be allowed to take some noncombatant work.

"What is it, Dodo, what's 'dissip—'" Wolfie was trying to snatch the paper, annoyed by the long words of it.

This could all take rather a long time and I won't be allowed to see you, nor anyone, nor allowed to leave here until it's over.

I'm glad that Spud was sensible and sent you to the country, and thrilled that you have a horse. Wolfie, it is a miraculous thing to watch a horse grow. They do it almost before your eyes—they build bone and muscle fast—at almost three pounds a day. Run your hands up and down his legs, handle him as much as you can. Halter him within two weeks, start to train him at four. Talk to him all the time, it will make him happy and a happy horse is a most wonderful companion.

I'll write to you often.

With all my love,
Pa

"Is he coming? When is—?" Wolfie was beside himself.

"No, Wolfie."

Dodo wound an arm around his shoulder.

Charged. Offense. Disciplinary procedure. Suspicion. Questioned.

The words shook in her head like knives. Pa? An "offense"? *Pa?* What had he done?

"But is he coming? Didn't he say he would come?"

"No, Wolfie, not for a while."

"But is he going back to fight?"

"No . . ."

After a few minutes, Wolfie said, "I *do* do that, I do talk to him, all the time."

Chapter Nine

Two days passed.

Dodo, who'd begun to enjoy school and whose drawing was thriving under Miss Lamb's tutelage, became more friendly with Chrissie Causey, though she talked to no one about Pa. To whom could she talk? she wondered, perhaps Miss Lamb, but everyone here seemed to know everything almost before it had happened and everyone was related to everyone else, so perhaps it was safer after all to talk to no one.

She was grateful Wolfie had only the vaguest notion that anything was wrong. His conviction that Pa was beyond the reach of all petty things was immutable as the stars.

Dodo ate little at breakfast, taking her bowl quietly to the sink and emptying it. She was keen to leave the house before Mary came. Mary might bring the post, but the ferrety look of her eyes, sharp and deep set in the smooth, shapeless face, made Dodo wary of her. She reached for her coat, pulled down Wolfie's too, and his cap. If they left now, they'd get away before Mary came.

"Hurry, Wolfie," she said from the door, but Mrs. Sprig's pony whinnied and there was an answering whinny from the lane. Mary dismounted, left her pony in the yard, untethered, and shouldered her way past Dodo into the house.

'Marigold! Marigold!' Mary scowled at Dodo, holding out a newspaper in the approximate direction of her cousin. "I told you, Marigold, told you it was dangerous." Now she was stabbing the paper with a plump forefinger. "Just don't know what you've got in your house." Mary lifted her chin and waited as Mrs. Sprig bent her head over *The Daily Mail.* Mrs. Sprig looked up eventually and stared at the children in silence. Wolfie and Dodo tried to see what was in the paper.

"Now sit down, Marigold," said Mary. "You'll be wanting a cup of tea." Mrs. Sprig let the paper fall to the floor and looked up at Mary, round-eyed with horror.

There on the first page was a picture of Pa, of him and Ma on the day they married, and another, smaller picture beneath it, of Pa with his medal. Wolfie's face brightened with sudden joy. He snatched up the paper.

"Let them have it," said Mrs. Sprig quietly.

Dodo was dragging Wolfie to the door. Waiting beside it, Mary shut it meaningfully behind them. On the porch, Wolfie gazed at Pa, at his calm smiling eyes, at Ma.

"'Hero Turned Deserter,'" Dodo mouthed. "'VC Held Under Close Arrest in Barracks. Soldier, Scholar and Cavalry Ace to Face Questioning by Military Police.'"

Chapter Ten

What had happened at Dunkirk? What had Pa done? Dodo asked herself for the hundredth time. She kicked pebbles as she walked. "Deserter"? *Pa?* Still reeling with the shock of it, she was silent. She'd not read the article to Wolfie, and he was now distracted by thoughts of Hero again.

"I've got some sweet rations left, Dodo, I'll buy you a sweet," offered Wolfie as they approached the village. "When I buy the honey, I'll buy you a Torpedo and a card for Pa."

Dodo gave him a brief smile.

"I'll tell him that Hero is quick at standing up but doesn't know how to lie down yet. And that he likes his neck scratched."

Dodo thought about Mrs. Sprig, about how awkward it would be to go back to Hollowcombe. What would Mrs. Sprig think about deserters? Would she be like Spud? But where else could they go? Pa was in his barracks and Spud was making balloons somewhere. She'd wanted to get rid of them, Dodo knew now, because of Pa. At the first whiff of a shadow over his name, Spud's loyalty had evaporated.

At the door to the Village Stores stood a roan mare loosely tied to a ring in the wall. Dodo tensed, seeing the pile of papers at the door, but it was only the *Western Evening News*, not *The Daily Mail*, and there was no picture of Pa on it. Wolfie inspected the mare, holding out his hand to her. He thought of Hero again and of something else he must tell Pa—that Hero wet his snout deeply in the milk. Pa had once said that a brave horse would always wet his snout deeply. The mare lowered her head to the small boy and, as Wolfie stroked the broad bone of her cheek, she closed her eyes at his touch, lowered her head, and seemed to sigh.

"A good sort," Wolfie announced loudly. "Pa would call that 'a good sort.'"

Dodo waited outside. She saw the church tower, grey and stern, the feathered ferns that nestled and roosted in the crevices. Beyond the old packhorse bridge, winding down the purple and gold common, was a troop of Home Guard. Like overgrown school-boys, feet almost to the ground, they rode the dark hill ponies that were everywhere in these parts. Wolfie took no notice of ponies, Dodo mused. It was as though they were town pigeons or some other indifferent species. She, on the other hand, rather admired their ferocity and independence, their sure feet and rugged coats, but to her eye, they looked sweeter unmounted.

Wolfie was taking his time so Dodo peered inside.

Two women stood by the sacks of loose goods. They were silent, watching Wolfie. Wolfie, gloriously unaware, was on tiptoe by the shelf of canned goods, a hand reaching first to one sweet, then another.

"Come on, Wolfgang, hurry." She used the name she always used to sound most stern.

Wolfie was placing the sweets, six eggs, and a postcard on the counter. The woman at the counter folded her arms and smiled a grim smile at the two women by the sacks. Wolfie asked for a penny stamp. He fumbled for coins, then dropped a clatter of them on the counter. She waited with a portentous smile and the sighing forbearance of all the saints. On tiptoe, Wolfie separated out the coins and began to count them.

"One, two . . ."

Certain he'd counted right, he pushed the pile towards her, pocketing the rest.

"Come *on*, Wolfgang," called Dodo.

The shopkeeper watched, with folded arms, in silence. Wolfie, bewildered, looked up at her, then began to count the coins again.

"I will not," she began. "I, who have a husband and a brother in the army, will not accept the custom of families of deserters . . ."

"What's a 'deser—'?" began Wolfie.

Dodo rushed in and grabbed his arm. "Wolfie. Come *now*."

Wolfie pulled away. "But—"

"WOLFIE. COME ON."

"Come, come." A voice called from the back of the shop, where the Post Office scales were kept. Miss Lamb stepped out with a parcel in her hands.

"But I haven't got my sweets," said Wolfie to Dodo.

"And I will not take *your* money."

The cash drawer was slammed shut.

"Come, come," said Miss Lamb again. "He's a *child*, Mrs. Potter. You can't refuse to serve a child. You can't weigh the sins of the father on the son."

"I will not . . . ," began Mrs. Potter, then, seeing the speaker, hesitated.

"And how is your husband, Mrs. Potter?"

"How *are* things in the Catering Corps?" continued the calm and pleasant voice of Miss Lamb as Dodo dragged Wolfie out. She marched him past the roan mare, and onto the bridge.

"Is he injured? Is Pa injured?" Wolfie was asking as she pulled.

"No." Dodo stopped on the bridge, released his arm, and took his hand. They stood in silence for a while.

"Here, Wolfie!"

They looked up. It was Miss Lamb on the roan mare, her hand extended. "Here're your sweets and your card."

She smiled kindly, then urged the gentle roan mare into a trot.

Wolfie turned to Dodo. "He'll come down and see

us before he goes back to war, he'll see Hero, won't he, Dodo?"

She yanked him, swung him round to face her, her eyes burning. "He'll never go back, Wolfie."

"But have we won . . . ?"

She shook her head.

"Then why . . . ?"

"He ran away, Wolfie. He RAN AWAY."

Wolfie stared up at her for a few seconds, then shook his hand free of hers. She spun round and marched away. When she turned to call him, from the other side of the bridge, she saw his brimming eyes, the trembling lower lip.

"Isn't he brave anymore? Isn't Pa—?"

Dodo marched on. "Don't you see?" she said. "There's a punishment for running away . . ."

What the punishment was, Dodo wasn't sure, but there was something she dimly remembered, something too terrible to frame in her mind.

Wolfie stood alone on the bridge. His eyes were starry and fierce as he said, "No . . . No, he didn't. Pa wouldn't . . . ever."

Chapter Eleven

At the start of the school day everyone huddled round the stove, the room filling with the friendly fug of steaming wool. Dodo, as one of the few older girls, was helping Miss Lamb collect books and pencils from a storeroom. Wolfie dropped his satchel and hung it on the pegs where the Causey sisters stood whispering.

Miss Lamb rang the bell. Wolfie admired Miss Lamb. She wore tall lace-up boots and a tweed cape, and had what Pa called "a good, brave head," by which he meant a strong nose and high forehead. Pa was keen on noses and foreheads.

Dodo's face turned white. As everyone took their places cross-legged on the floor, smallest at the front, oldest at the back, she remained, frozen, by the door. Wolfie followed her eyes. On her peg, next to where Dodo's friend Chrissie Causey had been standing, was her schoolbag, the buckles undone, with a copy of the *Daily Sketch* poking out.

Wolfie watched Dodo all day, saw her eyes flicker

from her work to that bag on the peg. In the afternoon she sat a little apart from the rest of her age group, head bent over a drawing. She sat at the front, as close as she could to the teacher, and Wolfie knew that was because she felt safer there, that no one could say anything to her without Miss Lamb hearing. Wolfie was drawing a young horse. He didn't like drawing and, unlike Dodo, had no gift for it. If he did have to draw, he'd always draw a horse. Hero would whinny to him now when he heard Wolfie's step, and he was thinking of that, longing to be there, longing to hear that whinny.

At the end of the day Dodo stayed where she was, bowing her head deeply over her paper as everyone raced to collect bags and coats and rushed out. She looked up as Wolfie approached and, seeing that the room was empty, she said, "No one'll remember what Pa did once, no one will remember Moreuil Wood . . . They only know, Wolfie, they only know . . ." She broke off, her anger confused by so much that she didn't know. "They won't talk to me, Wolfie. No one'll talk to me . . ."

Wolfie saw her flashing eyes, heard the anger in her voice, and thought how her sunniness had gone, how she was a tangle of thorns, a box of darkness, all shredded inside.

"They'll call us names *everywhere* we go." She stared venomously at the bag on her peg, leaped up, and stormed over to it. In the empty schoolroom she unrolled the paper on the cooling stove and read in furious, halting words:

DISGRACE OF CAPTAIN REVEL.
OFFICER & V.C. UNDER SUSPICION
OF DESERTION

Dodo snatched up her bag and stormed out, Wolfie running along behind her, coat half on, half off, satchel unbuckled and trailing.

They stayed with Hero for a long while. Wolfie added an egg to Hero's bucket and stirred in some honey, hoping that the honey might take away the taste of goat. "See? He has a silver tip to his tail, and his eye is good and dark." Wolfie rumpled the soft milky skin of Hero's muzzle. "And a dark mouth. That's important for a grey."

Hero drank deeply and Wolfie looked on with pride. The foal didn't need the honey or the eggs anymore but it was kind to spoil an orphan who lived alone and had to drink goat's milk.

Dodo watched Wolfie, wondering what on earth would become of them both, where they'd go, who'd have them now, who would look after Hero.

Wolfie picked an old dandy brush off its nail by the door. It was soothing to brush Hero's soft coat, to see the particles of dust flurry in the slanting light from the door. If you brushed hard and kept brushing it felt as though you could brush away the things you didn't want.

Hero snuffled Wolfie's shoulder, enjoying the attention.

"A girl, a boy, a young horse, a father under arrest," Dodo said to herself.

At dusk they made their way back to Hollowcombe. Mrs. Sprig was waiting in the low porch.

"Go upstairs." Seeing the look in her eyes, Dodo urged Wolfie on, pushing him past Mrs. Sprig.

"No, he'll stay and hear what I've to say and no harm it'll do him," said Mrs. Sprig, backing up to the door. "I'll not turn you out tonight, but I'll be seeing the billeting officer and she'll do what she can with you . . . I'll not have you staying here and have people thinking badly of me for giving charity—"

"It's not charity!" Dodo burst out. "Father and the government give you an allowance of ten shillings and sixpence for keeping each of us."

"I don't need it and I'll not have my son insulted by you being here."

"We'll not risk your reputation by staying, Mrs. Sprig. We'll leave in the morning," said Dodo elegantly.

"But . . . ," Wolfie was hissing, stricken, his eyes filling, "we *can't* . . ."

* * *

In the morning Mrs. Sprig was a tornado of tidying and straightening things as if to purge her house. Two suitcases stood ready at the door.

"Get your hair brushed and your coats on."

"But where?" asked Wolfie. "Where're we going?"

"Where you end up's no concern of mine. Where I'm taking you, in the first instance, is to church, then to the billeting officer."

Wolfie and Dodo, who carried her own suitcase, held hands, walking slowly behind Mrs. Sprig, who swung Wolfie's bag determinedly to and fro. Dodo cringed as they walked through the village, ashamed to be seen escorted away like this, bags in hand.

"Hero," whispered Wolfie at the old bridge. "He—he hasn't—the milk . . ."

They trailed behind Mrs. Sprig into the churchyard. Wolfie nudged Dodo, grateful to see Miss Lamb's roan mare tethered at the gate. They went up the path between the sheep that nibbled amidst the gravestones—marvellous sheep with deep hill-country coats and ancient faces. Mrs. Sprig dropped Wolfie's bag in the porch, as if relieving herself of something distasteful. Leaving hers beside it, Dodo followed her inside. The church was half full, the service not yet begun. Mrs. Sprig ushered them sniffingly to one pew, establishing herself, in a bustling, noisy sort of way, in another, farther forward. She fell at once to her knees, sighing and bowing her head deeply.

"There," whispered Dodo, seeing the tweed cape. "Miss Lamb's at the organ."

A priest with a white beard and walrus whiskers crossed the transept, bowed his head, turned and gave a brief introduction, his eyes alive with intelligence and humor. During the sermon Wolfie dug in his pocket, found Captain, and placed him beside his hymnal.

After the last hymn was announced, "O God, Our Help in Ages Past," and the priest had given the blessing, they filed out with the rest of the congregation, their heads bowed. On the porch Dodo collected their cases and they walked down the path, between the sheep and gravestones, towards the gate. Halfway between the gate and the porch, three figures, a family group, were standing in wait on the path: Mrs. Sprig's cousin Mary, arm in arm with what must be her husband, and, beside them, Ned Jervis. So *Mary* was Ned's *mother*! The father was as white-haired as his son, but more meanly made, the whole of him lean as a whip. Mary's darting gimlet eyes glittered with venom. Dodo and Wolfie stopped before the sinister trio. Mary whispered to her husband, who gave the merest nod in return, and moved, awkward, lame-legged, a step forward. Ned hung back.

Dodo continued tentatively, Wolfie at her side. Mr. Jervis stepped forward and spat. The vicious bauble fell by Dodo's shoes. Dodo and Wolfie recoiled in shock. Behind them, Mrs. Sprig and the priest, deep in talk, facing each other, had seen nothing. Dodo took Wolfie's hand and turned her back on the Jervis family.

"I'll not have them back," Mrs. Sprig was saying to the priest. "Your daughter assists the billeting people, she can . . ."

"Well, Mrs. Sprig, I'm sorry you feel you cannot help these two children . . ."

"Henry'd feel insulted—when he's out there doing his bit for his country, for his God . . ." Mrs. Sprig was visibly swelling, inflating with pride and indignation.

Miss Lamb came out of the church into the shade of the porch and took the elderly priest by the arm. "They must come, mustn't they, Father, to Lilycombe?" She stepped into the sunlight. "We ourselves are not so Christian, are we, that they can't stay with us?"

"No, Hettie, we are not," he answered, smiling at his daughter. His voice rose and he added, clear and sure as a bell, "*I don't, in fact, see that the Christian faith and warmongering can so easily share a house.*"

Wolfie crept up to Miss Lamb.

She took him by the hand and said, "Would you like that? Would you come to us?"

Wolfie, standing on tiptoe, whispered back, "I've got a horse."

"Be quiet," said Dodo.

Miss Lamb smiled again, amused. "Well, your horse must come too."

"You'll find your eggs missing—and other things." Mrs. Sprig was shifting, discomforted to find her cause not so readily embraced by the church as she'd expected.

"Petticoat government. I do what Hettie says." Father Lamb's blue eyes twinkled.

"Do you have eggs?" inquired Wolfie.

They set off down the path towards the gate, a deflated, diminished Mrs. Sprig following behind. There were no Jervises on the path now to bar their way.

"And what is Hero?" asked Father Lamb, placing a hand over the saddle of the roan mare.

"My horse. He's going to be a cavalry horse. He might be a Scots Grey."

"I see. And why's he called Hero?"

"Because Pa is a hero but the newspapers say he isn't anymore and no one will talk to us."

"I see. And where's Hero now?"

"He's hiding in a barn," said Wolfie.

"Not 'hiding.' *Hidden*," hissed Dodo, nudging Wolfie to silence him.

"At Windwistle."

When they reached the gate, Father Lamb paused while Miss Lamb tucked a Bible into her father's saddlebag.

"He likes condensed milk," said Wolfie.

"Well, now I know. You've a Scots Grey with a very sweet tooth hidden in a barn." Father Lamb was

88

smiling as he eased himself onto the roan mare. "Come along, Sunday"—he caressed her ears—"matins in the next parish." He waved to his daughter. "Hettie, Sunday and I will deliver matins, and be home for lunch."

Rough grazing stretched right to the walls of Lily-combe. Sheep-bitten smooth as a lawn in parts, in others embroidered with gold gorse, it lay like an altar cloth before a long, low stone house. There was no boundary, no fence, only the mown path along which they walked. A tangle of rugged hill ponies, each almost identical in marking, ran alongside in a wild scuffle. Dodo paused to admire them. A young one, ears flat, eyes wide with suspicion, cowered belly down, mealy nose flaring, like a light against its dark bear-like fur, then suddenly shied away, snorting.

"They're wild as birds," said Miss Lamb, laughing. "Unbroken, untamed. True wild horses." She laughed again as the pack plunged and wheeled away as one, tails and manes streaming. Surefooted as mountain goats, lissome as hawks, creatures from another, older world, they pounded over the turf, and dropped below the curve of the hill into a rough cleave.

"There's only fifty of them left now," said Miss Lamb. "Only fifty on the whole moor." She shook her head sadly. "Some say they're being poached, perhaps being taken for food."

Dodo looked at her in horror. *For food?*

They walked on in silence towards a long, low whitewashed house. A dishevelled, elderly rose draped itself comfortably over the porch, beneath which sat a huge dog, grey and tall. Miss Lamb whistled—a good masculine whistle. Wolfie turned in admiration. The dog paid no attention, but a sturdy biscuit-colored mare trotted up, tossing her head, whinnying.

"Scout doesn't think much of the ponies. She's rather above them and grazes only on the old tennis court." Miss Lamb dug a carrot out of her cape. Scout nuzzled her shoulder, then lowered her whiskery head to the carrot.

"Do you ride her?" asked Wolfie hopefully.

Miss Lamb shook her head. "I grew out of her a while ago," she said. "But Lilycombe will always be her home. She's a kind and compassionate lady, is old Scout, a brood mare through and through." She placed a hand on the dog's head. "Hello, Dreadnought," she said.

The dog looked straight ahead, unblinking, upright and dignified as Father Lamb's church tower. As though it were the most natural thing in the world, Scout was unlatching the front door with her nose. Wolfie gawped. Scout entered, negotiating, head lowered, the single stone step with care. Miss Lamb followed. Dodo and Wolfie hesitated on the porch, holding their suitcases.

"Can we live here?" whispered Wolfie, open-mouthed, to Dodo.

Dodo glimpsed a hall. Piles of books stood floor to ceiling, canvases stacked one against another.

"She went in—Scout—the horse . . . ," began Wolfie, wide-eyed.

"Oh yes—she used to hunt, you see," said Miss Lamb, emerging with a small basket, "and the hunt like to take the shortcuts through the house, rather than going round it, so she thinks it's normal and of course she discovered the larder once on the way through, so now—"

"Can we live here, Miss Lamb?" asked Wolfie.

"I very much hope you will, and when we're here, call me Hettie. Now, leave your cases there. Egg, did you say? Honey? And will condensed milk suit your charger, do you think?"

Chapter Twelve

Father Lamb sat by the fire, his dog at his side. Dreadnought was a hound of such dignity as to betray interest in nothing other than his master, not even in the young horse that stood near the sink. Father Lamb, however, glanced, over half-moon glasses, from Wolfie, lining up jars of honey on the draining board, to Hero. He looked the foal over, from head to tail.

"You'll make a milksop of him," he said. "He'll *not* grow up to be a horse. If he consumes more fresh dairy in a morning than Kensington sees in a month, he'll never be a horse, especially if he grows up in a kitchen . . ."

Wolfie beamed. "Look, Father Lamb, he's losing his baby fur. His hoofs are hard and he's too heavy to carry now."

Father Lamb's eyes were still on Hero as the foal explored the surface of the table with his muzzle, then the door to the larder. "Most of England hasn't seen a fresh egg since '39, yet your charger takes a breakfast egg *daily*."

"Not tomorrow," said Wolfie. "No more eggs. Four weeks old." He beamed again and moved the honey to the sideboard. Hero's head turned, monitoring the process of the honey. Hettie left what she was busy with at the Primus stove and went to light the copper in the washhouse for the hip bath. Dodo watched her carefully, concern in her expressive eyes.

"Bedtime," said Hettie, "for the three of you. The Invasion Committee'll arrive soon and perhaps we can persuade Hero to make way for everyone." She tightened the blackout curtains over the sink, lit her father's lamp, and adjusted the light-guard over it. Dodo put down her sketch pad.

The door to the yard opened and Samuel, the first member of the Committee, appeared, running and breathless. Samuel was always in and out of Lilycombe, doing odd bits and pieces on the land.

"Lower your lights. Bombs on this side," he urged. "Listen, antiaircraft guns—Jerry's close tonight—over the Channel somewhere."

"Up to bed," said Miss Lamb. "I'd like Hero in the boot room now, please, Wolfgang." Wolfie walked as slowly as he could towards the back door, Hero following, like a dog. Dodo tidied Wolfie's sticky plate and spoon and dragged him from the boot room where Hero was currently stabled. They went upstairs as the back door opened and more men arrived.

"The water'll be ready now," called Hettie.

"I don't want a bath." Wolfie was predictable about

93

baths. "Shall we tell Pa we don't want to come to London?" he asked, adjusting Captain on his bedside table so that his head faced Wolfie's pillow. "That *he* must come *here*?"

Dodo was silent, then she said, "Wolfie, it might be a long time till Pa can see us."

She'd sent a card to Pa's barracks, another one to Spud, telling them both of their new address and of how much happier they were. Wolfie, too, had sent Pa a card giving Hero's height in hands and his current dietary requirements. He'd left a note, too, on the barn door at Windwistle saying "GONE TO LILY-COMBE." Dodo wondered about the milk—about its arrival at Lilycombe every morning—she wondered if it were brought by Ned Jervis, and if his mother, Mary Jervis, knew. She wondered, too, whether Pa had written to the Lambs: They seemed to know a lot about Pa now.

A while later, half thinking about Pa, half listening to the rattle of antiaircraft guns and unable to sleep, Dodo crept to the window. From the first-floor windows at Lilycombe you could see the Bristol Channel and sometimes all the way to Wales. There was a red glow, far away, at the mouth of the Channel. Above it, searchlights scraped the dark. Bombs were falling somewhere.

No one talked to her at school now. Chrissie Causey no longer sat next to her. Dodo minded it all a little less since moving to Lilycombe, though she would never go into a shop again unless she was with Miss Lamb. Did Pa guess that people would be cruel to them? she wondered. Did he know that Spud had forced them out of Addison Avenue, did he suspect that their leaving Hollowcombe had anything to do with him?

She watched the searchlights, crossing and criss-crossing, and hypnotic. The droning had grown in volume, the planes must be close. Suddenly there were bombs falling nearby, the floors of the house rattling as in an earthquake. Wolfie was calling to her, reaching out to the bedside table for Captain. She took his hand and they crept halfway down the stairs, shivering, and sat listening to the voices beyond the door, thinking of the fire in there, of the comfort of being in there.

"That's over two hundred incendiaries," Father Lamb was saying. "Close."

Dodo and Wolfie shifted down another step towards the door. "Who has the Minute Book? Good. Note. Twenty shovels," Samuel was saying. "Twenty spades. Ten pickaxes. Ten wheelbarrows."

"How many horses?" said Father Lamb.

The roar of the planes was dimming.

"Thirty." Samuel's voice.

There was a pause, as the figure was noted down, then Father Lamb spoke again. "How many carts in the village?"

"Five."

"Five carts. Good. Next item."

"Plans for burial of the dead?" someone asked.

Wolfie wriggled under Dodo's arm like a puppy. As he did so, the small lead horse fell from his lap. It tumbled from step to step, clanked against the door at the bottom and came to rest.

A chair scraped, the door opened, and the children were revealed in a pool of yellow light. Father Lamb paused, then stooped to pick up Captain. Tenderly he turned the figure over in his hands, pulled the door to a little way, then climbed the stairs and sat beside them. Studying Captain thoughtfully, he was silent for a few minutes. Then he looked up and said, "Your father's as brave a man as ever walked this earth. It takes all kinds of courage, you see, to lead a good life. It takes great courage to lead a cavalry charge into firing guns but it takes courage, too, to go against what other men do and say and think. It's always easier to do what everyone else does. But it's this second kind of bravery, the not thinking what others think, that it takes to lead a good life."

Wolfie didn't really see at all but he liked being talked to as if he weren't a child and he loved to hear talk of Pa. Father Lamb led them upstairs. At their door, once Wolfie was in bed, Father Lamb placed a hand on Dodo's head.

"Will you help guard Hettie's herd? Two more were gone this morning, taken for God knows what . . . It's taken twenty years to breed that herd and it'd break her heart if . . ."

Dodo nodded.

"God bless you," he said. They listened to his tread on the stairs as he returned to his Invasion Committee.

Chapter Thirteen

Wolfie tugged at the string on the parcel. He scrabbled through layers of brown paper. A letter fell out. He handed it to Dodo and continued unwrapping.

Dodo read:

Britannia Barracks
Mousehold Heath

Darling Wolfie, Darling Dodo,

Spud found this in one of Ma's cupboards and she sent it to me to send to you. She thinks and I think too that you might have fun with it. Take good care of it—it reminded Ma of the holidays she spent on the moor—it was her father's—your grandpa's— when he was Master of one of the packs where you are.

Wolfie, tearing through sheets of newspaper, unearthed a bugle, shiny as the day it was made. He took it, put it to his lips, and blew.

Last night and the night before, immense numbers of enemy planes filled the sky over London, like storm clouds. Fire engines were everywhere. White smoke ballooned over the East End. I'm glad you're both safe and far away.

I've made my statement and now I have to wait for the Army's decision. These things can take a long while in wartime and everything is more difficult in this case because there are no witnesses—because no one except me saw what happened. Things may get public and nasty. Please take no notice of newspapers, you must learn to look and think for yourselves, never to be affected by what other people say or write.

Your loving
Pa

PS Wolfie: Does Hero have a dark muzzle? A grey horse always looks finer with a dark muzzle. Place your head against his and breathe with

*him. In with him and out with him. Be at one
with him.*

"Of course he has a dark muzzle," said Wolfie indignantly, his mouth to the bugle. "Dodo, you must paint him for Pa, you must do his portrait so he can see."

Chapter Fourteen

Father Lamb always made breakfast. In his dressing gown, he'd prepare Camp coffee and stand with a steaming bowl of it at the window that looked down towards the churchyard. He turned and took Wolfie's bugle down from the lintel and blew it to announce that breakfast was ready, then turned back to the window and his coffee.

Wolfie rushed downstairs and raced across the kitchen to the yard window, whistling to Hero. The sun shone out of a cobalt sky but the ground was stiff with frost. A fringe of glistening icicles hung like dinosaur teeth from the stable roof. Hero was now tall enough to reach his neck over the stable door, and would always be there, watching the kitchen door, waiting for Wolfie. Hero now shared the same winter quarters as Scout, though they were separated by a stall. Scout would rest her whiskery head on the wooden bar, following Hero's every movement with her gentle amber eyes. She never looked out into the yard, her eyes were always on Hero. Wolfie didn't approve of Hero being in a stable. He said that Hero missed the prancing and the chasing he could do outside. Wolfie turned from the window and went to the larder, saying, "Hero will have apples today and celery and a carrot. That's his Christmas treat. But he does not like to be in a box. He is restless in a box."

Thoughts of Hero always came with thoughts of Pa: Hero would have carrots and apples and celery for Christmas, but what would Pa have? Wolfie left the larder and joined Father Lamb at what they called the church window.

"You see, Wolfie"—Father Lamb gestured down to the churchyard where you could pick out, through mist that still clung to the hollows, the white sheep and the gravestones—"there'll not be far for me to go when the time comes, only Hettie's red currants between me and the grave." Father Lamb smiled. "Beneath that rowan there, all red and silver, is where I'll lie . . . The rowan, you see, is not only the tree of the moor, but also the tree that stands sentinel at heaven's gate."

It took Wolfie a minute or so to digest the thought of Father Lamb lying beyond the red currants, below the sheep and the rowan. He looked at Father Lamb's rosy cheeks and white beard and decided that he was not entirely serious. Eventually he took Father Lamb's hand and asked, "What do you do if you are in your barracks on Christmas day?"

"We've not heard from your pa for a while, have we? We'll pray for him today." He put an arm around the boy's shoulder, rumpling Wolfie's thick hair. "Will you ever be tidy, you tatterdemalion child?"

Wolfie looked up at him, bewildered.

"Must you always look as though you've slept the night in a manger, with the ass and oxen?"

"I will . . . ," began Wolfie, patting ineffectually at his hair.

"Come the Resurrection," said Father Lamb with a smile.

The door opened and Samuel entered. There was no day of rest for Samuel.

"They've gone, sir, two more gone. They were down in the cleave and they've gone—young ones—two fillies."

Father Lamb buried his face in his hands. After a minute he looked up and said, shaking, "Well, Wolfie, we'll not tell Hettie today, I think, nor Dodo." To Samuel he said, "Who's taking them? They're obstinate as camels—who is it do you think? It's surely a local?"

Samuel shook his head. As he turned to the door, he saw an envelope on the mat that he'd missed in his rush.

"We'll guard them every day," Wolfie was saying. "Every day when we're not at school."

Samuel handed the envelope to Father Lamb. Wolfie leaped forward.

"Is it another one from Pa?" There was a Christmas card from Pa waiting to be opened on the table.

Samuel glanced at Father Lamb, shaking his head. "It came by hand."

Father Lamb put the envelope on the Christmas breakfast table with the small group of envelopes that waited there. He embraced Samuel and wished him and his family a merry Christmas.

When Hettie and Dodo joined them, the fire was lit, the boiled eggs ready and waiting. Father Lamb said nothing about the missing ponies.

"It's lucky Hero's not a London horse, isn't it?" Wolfie said as he ate his egg. "London horses don't get honey and eggs."

Hettie took an envelope from the pile on the table. "Ten pints is a lot of milk for one horse in a time of war and rationing," she said. "Please teach him to be a normal horse and eat hay."

Dodo thought it would be better when Hero ate hay, if the milk had to come from the home of Mary Jervis. Mary Jervis delivered the mail to Lilycombe, but she left it in the porch outside, never coming in as she had at Hollowcombe.

Hettie read the card and stood it up on the table, picking up the envelope beneath.

"At least he doesn't eat eggs now," Dodo said.

"Do you think Pa gets eggs . . . ?"

Wolfie's voice shook a little and Hettie interrupted.

"Look, there's one for you both," she said, smiling. "And another. You open this one, Wolfie."

"From Pa," said Dodo, opening hers, and reading it out to Wolfie:

Dearest Dodo and Wolfie,

There are two small presents from me under your tree, but I know for you, Wolfie, the best present of all will be the moment your horse lays his head on your shoulder. There is nothing on earth like the moment a horse rests his head on your shoulder. Does Hero lay his head on your shoulder? For you, Dodo, I have something very special that once belonged to Ma.

Have the happiest day. I wish I could be with you and see you opening your presents.

With all my love to you both, Pa.

When Dodo looked up, Wolfie's lip was wobbling. In his hand he held a greetings card with a sprig of holly on the front. On the inside there was no writing, only a newspaper cutting pasted across both sides. A photograph showed Pa with the King, the medal in the King's hands. Wolfie looked up, fighting back his tears, let the card fall and leaped up from the table, pushing the door open and running out across the yard, ice splintering under his feet.

"For the love of God, on today of all days?" Father Lamb said again, taking it and reading it to himself:

SHAME OF A WAR HERO
CAPTAIN REVEL TO BE CHARGED
WITH DISOBEDIENCE AND DESERTION.
CASE CONTINUES.

Wolfie grappled with the icy bolt of the stable door, and fell sobbing into Hero's box, a flood of grief and pain erupting over him. Hero nudged Wolfie, almost throwing him off his feet. The two of them stood, nose to nose, Wolfie smiling now, weakly, through his tears. Like Eskimos they rubbed noses, exchanged breath, Wolfie blowing into Hero's nostrils, Hero's milky breath escaping in puffs over the tears on Wolfie's cheeks. "*Learn him by heart*," Pa had said in one of his letters. "*Learn your horse by heart*." Wolfie tangled his fingers into the deep grey mane, ran them along the ridge of Hero's back. He breathed the sweet apple scent of straw and hay and breathed deep and laid his head against Hero's chest, letting his breath rise and fall, rise and fall with Hero's. The tears dried on his cheeks, the raging and the churning inside of him calmed.

Scout paced restlessly along the wooden bar, returning to the spot closest to Hero, then pacing again.

When Wolfie looked up, Father Lamb was there, his arms resting on the stable door.

"Wolfie . . . ," he began.

Wolfie hung his head, fighting for words. Finding none, he reached for a glistening icicle and snapped it violently. He held it in his bare hands, the cold of it sticking and burning his hands raw. "They've taken it away, haven't they? The King—he's taken Pa's medal away." His eyes were two swollen pools and his voice croaked.

Father Lamb turned the boy towards him and placed a hand on each shoulder.

"Wolfie," he said, "what your pa did was immensely brave. In what will be perhaps the last cavalry charge in history, he led his men through *two* lines of machine guns—did that not once, but twice. He galloped at those guns with nothing but a lance."

Hero swung his head and nuzzled the boy for attention, his breath on the boy's neck.

"That takes unimaginable bravery. Whatever happens now, what he did that day, what he won that day, can never be taken away. A Victoria Cross can never be taken away, whatever happens."

Chapter Fifteen

Father Lamb sat in an old chintz chair by the door, a pink blanket over his knees, a sermon on his lap, his white beard and whiskers luminous in the sun, the first green of spring glimmering in the elderly rose over his head. Dreadnought sat at his side. Hettie patrolled her currant bushes, picking off caterpillars for her bantams. She favored benign neglect, in both housekeeping and horticulture, in every respect other than the currant bushes. Dodo was in the kitchen busy with a sponge cake for the afternoon moss-collecting expedition, cocoa, flour, and milk to replace chocolate.

Through the window she watched Wolfie criss-crossing the ground in front of the house. Hero followed Wolfie, and Scout followed Hero, jealous muzzle to his flank. Dodo smiled sadly to herself. Not a day went by without Wolfie writing to Pa. She pulled a letter out of her apron. Wolfie's letter formation was higgledy and picturesque. A small pencil drawing, meant to illustrate the scale of Hero's physical perfection headed the letter, beneath it Hero's height in hands, then:

Dear Pa,

Hero always swings his tail. That's the sign of a happy horse, isn't it? His tail is long now and he doesn't have his baby fur anymore. He eats only grass and hay now and is very pleased with himself.

Love, Wolfie

PS I hope you can come soon.

The mysterious buckets of milk had stopped coming after Wolfie wrote a message and pinned it to the stable door: I EAT HAY NOW. Dodo had been relieved about that because the milk probably came from a boy whose parents had spat at them. She'd asked Hettie about Ned, and Hettie told her that Ned had had to leave school early, that he'd had to take full-time work; his father's leg had worsened and he was unable to work.

"He does what he can, takes bits and pieces of work wherever he finds it. It'll be a struggle for him to keep hold of that farm . . . He never wanted to take it on, you know, he wanted to stay on at school, but his older brother died at Dunkirk in those first months of the war. He was always a clever boy, and kind." She had smiled at her. "Still, he'll be all right—he knows his way about. The peat water of this place runs in the Jervis veins—they know this moor like no one else and they take it as theirs."

Father Lamb had said that he feared that all the promise in Ned might wither under the strain of fending for his siblings, that he knew there were problems with the rent on the land.

Dodo looked out as she sifted flour. She looked at Wolfie—at the smile on his face, the hand in his pocket fingering, probably, an apple. Hero was starting forward, nuzzling Wolfie's pocket, now lifting his head, swinging his tail. *Look at me,* he was saying. *Am I not a fine horse?*

Pa wrote often from his barracks, mainly with advice for Wolfie, though sometimes there'd be bits about the progress on his case too. But still their understanding of what had happened at Dunkirk was partial and confused. Pa had written this week that he felt like a small boy standing in a corner of the classroom being punished for something he hadn't done. They'd smiled at that, but Dodo felt that she, too, was being punished for something *she* hadn't done, her love for Pa turning cloudy with anger and a sense of injustice. Wherever she and Wolfie went, they were watched in silence, and silence would cling like a shadow as they left; then there'd be the whispering. The Causey girls no longer taunted openly.

When Dodo came into the schoolroom they'd watch her in sinister silence, three dark witches that seemed to know something Dodo didn't, something too terrible for words. She'd caught anxious glances between the Lambs as though they, too, knew something, Dodo thought, that she didn't. If Pa were found guilty, would he go to jail, would that be the worst that could happen? The schoolroom tauntings angered and outraged Wolfie, but at Lilycombe he could forget. For Dodo there was no such rest, and the dark knot of fear inside her grew and spread its web.

She looked out the window onto the purple sweep of the common. She'd first admired, now loved, the savage beauty of these hills, each day the leafy whiteness and brightness of Holland Park receding further from her mind.

Hero whickered and was answered by a whinny from Scout. Dodo smiled. Hero stopped and stretched, allowing Scout to nibble and caress him. He took her love as no more than his due and was sometimes domineering, sometimes loving and protective of the wise and gentle Scout. Now he tossed his head and cantered playfully away, his legs springy and dancing, improbable as a daddy longlegs. Scout cantered after him, the two of them dodging the flowering may trees, dodging gorse. Wolfie was watching and smiling, the bugle in his hand winking and flashing in the sun.

Hettie joined Dodo at the window and together they looked out.

"Scout thinks of nothing but Hero. He is a prince to her," said Hettie, shaking her head and smiling. After a little while, seeing Dodo so quiet, she said, "Scout's yours, Dodo, to ride, for as long as you're here. Scout would love to be ridden and I would love you to ride her. You'll come to no harm with her, she knows the moor better than anyone, it's in her blood."

"Oh—!" Dodo was too moved to speak, overcome with joy and gratitude.

Hettie smiled and began to collect provisions for the afternoon's expedition, raising her head again to look out. "Why not ride her out today and lead Hero behind you on a halter and rope—what do you say?"

Dodo was dizzy at Hettie's kindness.

"Will you ride her? You'll love her—she's as sure-footed and lionhearted as any horse."

When Wolfie came inside, horse slobber in his hair, straw clinging to his jumper, he asked, "Why do we have to collect moss?"

"It's for dressings. The Red Cross needs a million dressings a month for the wounded."

"A million is a lot," said Wolfie.

"It grows right here, up on the moor. Sphagnum holds more than twenty-five times its weight in water, so you see, it can hold more blood than cotton can . . ."

The children were silent. Down here in the country, and especially so now that Pa was in England, the war felt far away. The distant rumbling over Bristol, Hettie's moss, and the Invasion Committee meetings were the only reminders that the country was at war.

Later, as they left, Wolfie said proudly to Father Lamb, "We're going to collect moss for the wounded. Hero is coming and Dodo's going to ride Scout."

"Good for you. Sphagnum stops infection," said Father Lamb. "Did you know that? The Highlanders, after Flodden, stuffed their wounds with moss. Up here, a wounded deer will drag himself to a sphagnum bog with his last breath because he knows it will help heal him."

"Bogs preserve men," said Wolfie unexpectedly. "I am learning about Bog Man at school. Ancient man used bogs to keep his butter fresh but Hero won't like bogs because he does not like to get his feet wet."

"And with good reason—water on the hills can be dangerous in these parts. Up on the Chains, the bogs can be twenty foot deep after rain."

"Scout will look after them," said Hettie. "Dodo will ride her there and Scout will carry the moss back in baskets."

"The soldiers need a million dressings a week," said Wolfie.

"A million. Is that so, Hettie?" Father Lamb looked up at his daughter. "A million a week?" He took off his glasses and rubbed his forehead. "Do you know, H. G. Wells says that every decision should be made in the presence of a wounded man, so that the War

Cabinet is reminded what war does. I think that's right, Hettie, I think that's right."

"When can I ride Hero?" asked Wolfie.

"Not yet," said Hettie. "But it's the first step, haltering him to Scout. Today we'll teach your proud emperor a thing or two."

Chapter Sixteen

"Prepare to mount . . . ," Dodo commanded. "Mount!"

The forbearing Scout waited as Wolfie scrambled up onto the saddle in front of Dodo. Hettie handed up a saddlebag, bulging with jam jar, magnifying glass, paint box, sketch pad, and lunch.

"Destination Pennywater," said Dodo to Wolfie. "Mission Pony Patrol."

Sun touched them that summer, alighting on their young and troubled lives, unexpected as a butterfly, and staying. After the foamy white hawthorn, the grassy slopes around Lilycombe had grown thick with yellow buttercups. Fear for Pa receded as endless sunlit days passed in a galloping succession. Pa had written that he thought the case against him might be dropped or forgotten since it seemed to be taking so long. There'd been nothing in the papers for a while and, for a time, the children found that out riding, with Scout, they could together forget and be free.

Almost every day they rode together on Scout, Hero

roped alongside, haughty as a captured princeling. The horses, Scout and Hero both, taught Wolfie and Dodo to love the place, to love the summer pink and purple hills, the silver rivers that laced the dark combes like streamers. In and out of cloud shadows, they wandered like will-o'-the-wisps, Hero ahead, frolicking, defiant, wild as a hawk, agile as a goat, the iron-grey tail a streaming banner. Above and far away, fighter planes flashed and winked like silver blades, unheeded.

Pennywater was their secret place.

Scout carried them down over the soft nibbled turf through musky clouds of gorse, to a stream, their stream, a stream that never ran dry, a hidden place of glittering amber water, that flashed between cushions of deep and dripping moss. Fizzy with curiosity or fear at each new thing, Hero followed, dainty on his butterfly legs.

Dodo settled herself on a rock and looked out for Hettie's ponies. They came to drink at Pennywater, for this was their place too. She stretched out, face to the dappled sun, listening to the sounds of sheep and water, waiting. After a while, she said, "Time passes more slowly here."

Wolfie, creeping toad-like along the bank, collecting creeping crawling things for his jar, paused to consider this.

"How does it?" His mind, more literal than hers, fought such an idea.

"Show me," said Dodo, reaching for the magnifying glass and jar.

She inspected his haul of buzzing and black things. "What will you *do* with them, Wolfie?"

"They're for the bantams," he replied, very proud. "They lay more if you give them bugs." He paused, looked up and said with a mayfly leap from one subject to another, "Pa's case will be soon, won't it?"

Dodo said nothing for a while, then, "Hettie says they are not laying so much now, she doesn't know why."

Wolfie stuck his chin out and lowered his eyes.

"Do you think of London much, Wolfie?" she asked later.

"No, I just want Pa to come here, I want him to see Hero—I want that every day."

Scout, tethered loosely to an arthritic withy tree, tugged at her rope. Dodo laughed fondly, knowing she was fretting for Hero.

"Look, there, he's just there . . ." She broke off and leaped up. "Look, Wolfie, the ponies—they're here."

They cantered in a dark and pounding clot, short-legged, clever as cats on the steep soft ground.

"Fifteen—there's only . . . I can only see fifteen," began Dodo.

Wolfie squatted and held the glass over his jar. "Why do they take them?" he asked, probing the contents of his jar with a blade of grass.

"I don't know . . . I don't like to think why they take them or where they take them."

She counted again with a trembling forefinger. She knelt and packed the remnants of the picnic away, snapped her paint box shut.

Hettie, surprised to see them back so soon, came out into the yard. She saw Dodo's face and asked quietly, "How many?"

Silently Hettie removed Scout's saddle. Dodo followed her into the tack room with the bridle.

"What're we to do? Must we have them in the house to keep them safe?" asked Hettie, running the tap, taking the bridle from Dodo to wash the bit. She bent deeply over the sink, and put a hand over her eyes. Dodo and Wolfie watched her in anxious silence. After a minute, she lifted her head. "They're born here, bred here, hefted to this hill, generation after generation . . ." After a little while, she turned with a visible effort and went to take a towel from a basket in the corner.

She paused, lifted the basket, and turned to them, holding it out and saying in a lighter, forced tone, "I was worried the bantams weren't laying and all this time they were, weren't they?"

Wolfie looked at the floor. Dodo looked at Wolfie,

stepped forward to the basket, then spun round to Wolfie.

"Wolfie," she said, horrified. "Wolfgang, you can't just help yourself! What were you planning on—?"

Wolfie was still staring at the floor. Dodo took his arm.

"Wolfie, what . . . ?"

"I'm saving them for Pa—for when he comes. You don't get fresh eggs in a barracks."

"Oh, Wolfie."

There were tears in Hettie's eyes. She put an arm around his shoulder and led him across the yard and into the house.

Father Lamb, sitting by the fire, looked up at Wolfie's grimy, guilty face.

"You must tell them, Father, you must tell them now," said Hettie. She held up the basket of eggs, two dozen or more, perfect and lovely as porcelain. "Wolfie's been hoarding eggs for when his father comes."

Father Lamb shifted a little in his chair, folded his glasses onto the table, and patted the arms of the chair, for them to sit on either side.

"What?" said Dodo, alarmed. "What must you tell us?"

"We've had a letter from your pa. It'll be a long time before he's able to see you, much longer than you or we thought." He waited a while. "You see, there're charges against him . . . As you know, desertion and disobedience are serious charges, very serious indeed, and the punishment can be—"

"Pa didn't run away," said Wolfie, quiet and furious, eyes burning. "He never would."

"No, Wolfie, I don't think he *would* run away, but you see there is no other witness. There is no one to speak on his behalf besides himself . . . He's going to be held in close custody while the charges are investigated. If the charges hold, there'll be a court-martial."

"What will happen?" asked Dodo.

"Where is he?" asked Wolfie at the same time.

"He's still in barracks and will stay there until . . . well, until he is tried by a court-martial."

"But what *is* a 'marshal'?" Wolfie asked, exasperated.

"A judge," said Dodo. "A very important judge."

"He'll write to you, but he wanted me to explain, because these things are complicated. But we must all—you must both—keep your faith in him, not believe what people say, what will be written. It may be"—he put an arm around each of them—"it may be some time before his trial, and a very long time before he's able to see you."

"If he *is* found guilty . . ." Dodo, white-faced, was unable to complete the question.

"He didn't, he never—" began Wolfie.

"If he *is* found guilty . . . well, we must pray that someone who was there, someone who saw it all, is still alive, is alive somewhere, perhaps a prisoner of war—if there was such a survivor, that man could come forward one day as a witness. In time, it *is* possible that—"

"What . . . !" Dodo was screaming. "What if no one is alive, what if no one comes forward, what if they find him guilty?"

Father Lamb said nothing. Hettie stepped into the loud silence and tried to draw Dodo to her, but Dodo was rigid in her arms, her head swelling with half-heard things, things she dimly remembered Pa once saying about the punishment for desertion in the last war, things the Causey sisters whispered noisily amongst themselves. And Dodo thought she knew, now, for certain, from the pain in Father Lamb's eyes, that the punishment for Pa, if he were found guilty, would be death.

Chapter Seventeen

Hettie cancelled the newspaper delivery.

Many letters came from Pa to the children, tender, fearless, and uncomplaining, then, in the autumn, a long letter came from him, addressed to Father Lamb. Father Lamb rose from the breakfast table and went to his study.

After what seemed a long while he called the children in. When he spoke, it was without reference to the letter, which lay to one side under his glasses on a walnut side table. Dreadnought sat beside him, unblinking, immovable as a statue, above noticing the unusual presence of children in his master's study.

"You must be brave in the days to come, Dodo, Wolfie." He looked from one to the other. "The national press have taken a great interest again in your father. There will be a court-martial. He will be tried and the case is likely to be very public. It may well drag on for some time and it may cast a cloud, perhaps forever, over his name—and over yours. He knows this and knows he owes it to you to tell you what happened."

The children drew closer to each other. Dodo took Wolfie's hand.

"I'll try to explain, as simply as I can, what he's written to me." Father Lamb rose, and took a deep breath. "When we pulled out of France, there was a terrific rush as our men raced to the beaches around Dunkirk, the enemy hot on their heels. Your father was in the rearguard, in command of a company. He arrived at a place called Wormhout, and was given orders to defend a farmhouse, to stay there and to hold it. When the enemy approached, they were to delay the Germans, to hold them off, so that as many of our men as possible could get to those beaches and get home.

"They held Wormhout for two days, until the last of our men had passed through. By midday on the third day, German troops were massing on the outskirts. Your father came under heavy fire from waves of German Stuka bombers. One by one, the Allied units holding the town withdrew until only three companies remained. The town was turned to dust and rubble. Their job had been done but they received orders to stay put, 'to hold their position to the last man and the last round.' Your pa and his men had only the rounds left in the Boys antitank rifle and the Bren gun, but they fought on, exhausted, hungry, trapped, and outnumbered.

"Again the orders were given from HQ to stay put, that a company of Norfolks would bring relief and ammunition. Still the German planes came in waves and waves."

Father Lamb turned from the window and looked at them both.

"Imagine what he felt as he looked at his men, three of whom had served with him in 1918, all of whom must have felt like sons or brothers. If they were to stay, they would face the choice of death or surrender. There would be no other option. Your father's men were to be sacrificed for no good reason. Nevertheless, they obeyed instructions and waited. Some time later a Major Vickers of the Cheshires, and two of his men, made their way along a ditch and into the farmhouse. Since Vickers was the more senior officer, he took command and instructed your father and his sergeant, Box, to go out and find the Norfolks. Your pa and Sergeant Box crawled along a hedgerow, to the position in which the Norfolks should have been. There they heard the sound of drunken laughter. They saw three German officers outside a barn. From inside the barn there was silence. Those weren't ordinary German officers, but officers of the SS. The SS—Dodo, Wolfie—are Hitler's personal guard.

"There's no gentle way to say what your pa found, later, inside that barn . . . The Norfolks had been killed—all of them—at point-blank range. They'd surrendered, that was clear because they were naked to the waist. The shooting of men that have surrendered goes against all laws of military conduct . . ."

Father Lamb paused, looking blindly out of the window.

"It was clear to your father that the SS were in command of Wormhout. If your pa and his men surrendered, they, too, would be massacred. He ran back and urged Vickers to retreat, to get the men away, to retreat if they could, but Vickers, quite simply, did not believe what your pa said he'd seen. Vickers said such a thing was impossible, that no massacre had happened. He instructed the company to stay and hold the position. Horrified at the fate that would befall his men, your father argued with Vickers and again urged both Vickers and his own men to leave. Vickers accused him of inciting cowardice and desertion. Your pa grew more forceful in his argument. Vickers said he had no choice but to report your pa to HQ. A report was filed against your father."

Father Lamb turned from the window and spoke directly to the children.

"In a desperate attempt to save the useless sacrifice of the lives of the men he loved, and thinking nothing of his own reputation, again your father begged his men to retreat. In front of his own men he was arrested, led at gunpoint to the dairy building, and locked in. A while later, with nothing but their bayonets to defend themselves against the flood of black tanks, Vickers surrendered. Through a window your pa saw the SS line his men up, strip them, and herd them into a barn. He heard the machine guns and he heard their cries."

Father Lamb's eyes clouded. "Later, much later, he managed to break out of the dairy and make his way to the barn. Every man was dead except Vickers, who was badly wounded. Your father dragged him out. For a while they lived off raw potatoes and water from puddles. At some point, a Frenchwoman took Vickers in and nursed him. Your pa made his way home through France, Spain, and then to England from Gibraltar. Nothing has been heard of Vickers."

Father Lamb knelt stiffly on the floor at their feet, took the letter, and read, "Wolfie, Dodo, I *did* encourage my men to retreat, I *did* disobey my commanding officer, I *did* incite desertion . . . But I did that for what I believed to be the right reason. Unless I can prove that the massacre occurred, there's little chance of my winning my case. Until the bodies of my men are found, there is only the hope that Vickers is alive somewhere and will one day prove my story. As far as I know, he is the only possible survivor."

Many letters followed, but it was what Father Lamb explained to them that day that helped Dodo's anger with Pa evaporate, that made Wolfie's pride in his father burn with a fiercer flame, that helped them both endure the private scorn, the public glare, that was to come.

Chapter Eighteen

Hettie propped Dodo's painting on the mantel. Wolfie, on the floor, amidst a heap of wrapping paper, was spellbound, as if seeing Hero for the first time, by the candor of his eyes, by the confidence, the assurance of the carriage of his head. How fast that baby face had changed. When had it become that of a beautiful young horse?

Wolfie held Pa's parcel in his hands. He'd saved that till last, but still he made no move to open it, spellbound by the beauty of his horse.

"It's not your brushstrokes he's so astonished by," whispered Hettie to Dodo. Wolfie longed, they all knew, to send the picture to Pa. Wolfie bit his lip, bent his head, and unfolded Pa's card.

Dear Wolfie,

You're ten today. I wish I could see you to know what you are growing up to be. Are you still the explosion of a child that you were? Do you still leap like a gadfly from one thing to another? Are you still impatient as the dawn? Be impatient with the world, Wolfie, but never be impatient with a horse.

It's not easy to find a present when you're under arrest but I'm proud to give you my saddlebag. This is the bag that Captain carried at Moreuil Wood. It's a fine bag to strap to the saddle of a fine horse to be ridden by a fine young man.

If you ride a horse with your heart and you believe you fight for what's right, nothing can stop you.

Ride from the heart, Wolfie, always ride from the heart.

With all my love,
Pa

Eventually Wolfie passed the bag to Dodo, his voice breaking as he whispered, "Captain wore this at Moreuil Wood."

"I've something for you, Wolfie," said Hettie. "Come."

She led him into the kitchen. On the table sat a saddle, the deep seat and skirt darkened and softened with years of oil, the cantle and knee roll in a lighter tan, the pommel polished as a chestnut. To the side lay a bridle, ribboned with a grey-and-white bow at the edge of the gleaming bit.

"We were lucky—this old saddle of Father's fits. Unless Hero grows much more, it'll last a while."

"Is he ready— Can I . . . ?" Wolfie leaped to the window. Father Lamb joined him and they looked out at Hero and Scout, standing muzzle to muzzle. Scout whickered gently at Hero, then resumed her nipping and grooming of him.

"Two years old, Wolfie, and he's already tall for you . . . He's going to be a horse to be reckoned with . . . but at two years he can be saddled."

Wolfie yelped for joy, flung open the casement, and whistled.

The horse raised his head and cantered between the snowy thorns, leaf light quivering over his flanks like stippling on water.

"Bring the saddle, Wolfie," said Hettie, taking two apples and chopping them. She slipped the pieces into Wolfie's pocket and picked up the bridle.

Wolfie leaped towards the saddle, his heart spinning like a Catherine wheel. He picked it up, staggering under the weight of it, and soldiered out across the yard.

That day Hettie and Wolfie began to break in Hero.

They took him to the lane where green glimmered in the beech hedgerows, Dodo ahead with Scout,

Wolfie leading the young grey horse, feeding him apple as he went. Day by day, they walked him through the magical dappled green of spring, a little more weight on his back each day. Hero's eyes blazed with outrage when the saddle was first placed on his back, but Scout was always at his side, steady and calm at his flank, so Hero accepted it. Later, he was astonished by the bit, outraged at the indignity of the bridle, but Wolfie whispered to him, and he listened with a willingness to co-operate born of the unqualified trust he had in the boy who'd slept at his side, who'd fed him honey on his fingers, drunk milk from the same bucket.

Later, free of the saddle, Hero would roll on the cool turf, watched tenderly by Scout. The games of his colthood, the fawn-like leaping and starting, were now outgrown, his movements grown rounder, more considered, more graceful. His chest had broadened, there was elegance in his stance, seriousness in his eyes, a patrician depth to his face.

If ever he stepped away from Scout, she'd squeal and he'd answer, standing kingly and tall, with the deep valley below, the purple curve of the common beyond.

He was shod in early June, and grew fizzy and proud at the sound of his feet clipping on the cobbles. He'd been an easy horse to break, Hettie said, because the trust he had in Wolfie was absolute.

Mounted for the first time on Hero, looking as accidental atop the tall horse as a piece of thistledown, pride shone, wide as sunlight, in Wolfie's smile. Dodo and he rode together, she on Scout, leading him on Hero. If she loosed the lead rope, Hero would sniff and skitter, dart sideways from leaves and breezes, leap to avoid water. His flickering ears would betray his ignorance, suspicion, or astonishment at everything, but as the summer ripened, his understanding of the world grew and he stepped out with confidence and pride.

When they cantered, for the first time, through golden brown grass waist high, laughter sprang from the boy like water from a spring. Hearing the boy's laugh, feeling the current of it in his own veins, Hero moved freely into a long, clean gallop, learning the strength he had in him, power surging inside, one ear turned as Wolfie's laughter rolled and tumbled and crested in a froth of joy. The boy's trust in the horse, the horse's trust in the boy, was each beyond question.

With Dodo and Scout they'd picnic in valleys ribboned with silver streams, the coat of the young horse silver as a moon in the leaf shadow. They'd ride to Hoar Oak, remote and fairy-tale, to watch the firing practice at Larkbarrow. They patrolled the ponies at Pennywater, or rode over the Common to watch the troops and tanks on maneuvers, or gallop across the high moor, through feathery tufts of cotton grass, sweet as summer snow.

If Hero had to stop and wait for Scout, he'd stamp and snort, and lift his head to survey the open grassland, proud as an eagle. Then Wolfie would blow his bugle, and they'd canter on. Driven by gossamer whims, arms lifted to the sky, reins loose, laughing, Wolfie raced clouds, raced birds that swirled like scraps of paper, laughing, forgetting, the mother lost in baby-hood, the father under arrest.

In late summer they rode through fire-gold sedge, leaping the still black water that stood between the rush grass. They galloped and galloped and gal-loped, through sun and rain and shadow, as though in and out of centuries, through time itself. The bracken blazed bronze-red, the beech leaves turned to golden coins that curled and darted and eddied down. Wolfie and Dodo would race, laughing, reaching out to them, each captured leaf treasured, good luck for Pa.

On their horses they came to know and deeply love the moor, in mist and mizzle, in the sudden storms that snapped new growth like a knife, in the violent surge of spring, in heady summer, in long, red autumn.

When the school year began again, they were forced once more into the uneasy company of their school-mates, once more caught by the scrutiny and suspi-cion of a close village community. At Lilycombe in the long autumn evenings, in the glow of the fire, they'd sit together, Dodo's head bent over *The Lives of Artists*, but creeping, from time to time, to the win-dow, to look suspiciously into the night, a soft crease on her brow, Hettie's ponies never far from her mind. Father Lamb, held in the golden halo of his oil lamp, would glance up and smile gratefully at her. Wolfie toyed with Captain, or wrote long notes to Pa. He'd sent Dodo's picture to Pa in the end, and Dodo hadn't minded, said she was proud to think of it in Pa's lonely room. Pa had written back to say that he'd thought no horse could live up to Wolfie's praise until he'd seen the painting. He'd advised, too, that Wolfie use soap flakes as the best way to get the mud off a grey horse.

In November, Wolfie asked, "Haven't they set a date for the trial?"

His voice quavered as he struggled to contain the flood of longing that could burst from time to time within him.

Father Lamb looked up from his sermon and shook his head. "It's still not been set . . . it seems there is no man willing to sit in judgment on your father, but a long delay's helpful to him, and perhaps they know that—there's more chance of a witness coming forward." He put his pen down and looked steadily at them both. "In any case, it wouldn't be right for you to think that you'll see him straight after—"

"Why?" began Wolfie.

Hettie looked up from the Red Cross parcel she was tying and glanced at her father sharply. "His record, the medal, all that will surely stand in his favor, Father, even if there's no witness?"

He nodded and addressed the children. "Yes, all that will, I am sure, stand in his favor. But if it doesn't, remember that he himself was prepared to pay the price of breaking the law in the hope of saving his men."

"If it doesn't go well . . . ," Wolfie said slowly.

Dodo bowed her head deeply over her book.

"He can appeal," said Hettie quickly.

At nine, she turned on the wireless.

"The German army in North Africa is in full retreat, after suffering a comprehensive defeat in Egypt at the hands of the Eighth Army under Lieutenant-General Bernard Montgomery."

Father Lamb leaped up, spilling his whisky. "Rommel's on the run—we've taken El Alamein—our first victory—this is our first victory." Father Lamb, child-like with glee, was hugging them all, now leading Wolfie to the map, as the radio news continued.

"Allied troops have captured more than nine thousand prisoners of war . . ."

Father Lamb was moving enemy pins out of Egypt.

"This is it, Wolfie! We've marched them forward and back, forward and back, for three years—but from now on, they'll never go back."

Wolfie mustered a smile.

Chapter Nineteen

Wolfie crept barefoot and on tiptoe to the front door. He pulled his dressing gown close around him, then eased up the iron latch. Mary Jervis and her pony delivered to Lilycombe first, leaving the mail in a wicker basket under the porch. There'd be a letter from Pa today, or soon, he was sure. Pa must know the date of the trial by now. Wolfie knew that, because he'd overheard Father Lamb whisper so to Hettie last night. He'd also said to Hettie, "If he can prove the massacres happened, then Wormhout will, one day, go down in history as one of the most horrific war crimes ever committed."

Wolfie started. Pinned to the cotton sprig lining of the basket was a carefully cut article from a newspaper. He bent, slowly, to the basket.

**SHAME OF A HERO. CAPTAIN REVEL:
COURT-MARTIAL SET FOR EARLY SPRING 1943**

Pa. He wouldn't see Pa till spring. Pa wouldn't see Hero till spring. Wolfie ripped off the cutting and screwed it into a tight ball in his pocket. His hand formed a fierce tight fist around the ball and he blinked furiously, valiantly, into the grey dawn, fighting the pricking in his eyes.

He said nothing to Dodo later because newspapers upset her and because Pa would tell them in a letter.

Chapter Twenty

One morning in April, Ned was waiting for them at the crossroads.

"I thought you'd like to know," he said simply, holding out a newspaper, the red of his cheek startling and violent in the cold.

Dodo shied away, fearful as a wild deer.

"They don't take papers anymore at Lilycombe an' I thought you'd want to know."

Wolfie took the paper and Ned turned and left. Wolfie started to read, in a halting voice. Nauseous with dread, Dodo turned away.

**CAPTAIN REVEL SENTENCED
FOR DESERTION AND INCITEMENT
TO COWARDICE
VC GETS TWO YEARS' IMPRISONMENT
WITH HARD LABOR.**

Dodo grabbed the paper, sobbing and choking with relief. Wolfie was stock-still, rigid with shock.

"Two years . . . Imprisonment," he whispered.

"It's all right, Wolfie, he's all right . . . Hard labor, prison . . ." She took him by the shoulders, smiling, her eyes sparkling through her tears. "Prison—but that's all."

"Sentenced . . . ," Wolfie stammered. "He wasn't . . . he didn't . . . he was—"

"It doesn't matter, none of it matters," she said.

"Two years?" repeated Wolfie in horror and disbelief.

"Come on. Pick up your bag," she said. "Let's not go to school today."

Wolfie, thinking of the newspapers, and everyone knowing, nodded silently.

They met Father Lamb on Sunday on the lane, on his way to tell them.

Two officers had refused to be jurors, he said, as they walked home together, arm in arm. Two more officers had been brought in. They too had refused. Any decent man would have trembled to sit in judgment on such a case, said Father Lamb, especially if they'd fought alongside Pa in the first war. The small print of the article, he said, was kinder than the headline. When they had finally found an officer to preside over the court, he'd been young and inexperienced, rushed in on the case by a callous bureaucracy, embarrassed by the long and public detention of a national hero. Pa had spoken in his own defense, the courtroom packed to the gunnels with men who'd served at one time or another with Pa in 1918.

The Times said there were tears in many eyes when Pa was sentenced.

Wolfie thought later that Ned must have pinched one of the papers from his mother's round. Maybe Ned knew about the cuttings in the basket and the Christmas card and perhaps he was trying to make amends for his parents.

The next day they received a brief note Pa had written outside the courtroom.

My darling children,

My war record did count in my favor. Two years will go fast. For the hard labor part of my sentence I have applied to work in the mines. I'd like the experience of doing that and from there I would be able to continue, at least in part, the work I was doing before the war.

I'm truly sorry only on account of you both. For myself, I'm not afraid, nor am I ashamed. I pray that you, too, will feel there was no shame in doing what I believed to be right. My head is, as the poet says, bloody but unbowed.

Your loving Pa

PS Wolfie: Does Hero look into your eyes? When a horse looks into a man's eyes it's as though he can see the very heart of you. There was a night at Moreuil Wood when I could scarcely look Captain in the eye because I knew for certain the strength of the German forces into which we'd ride the next day. Looking into Captain's eyes that night was far harder than any prison could ever be, and I am sure that Captain knew that night, what I knew, that he could see into the heart of me.

Later, from Wormwood Scrubs, where he'd been sent, he wrote that there was a good library, that a piece of good writing was a ray from heaven, and that the morning exercise was as good as a dram of whisky.

Chapter Twenty-One

Every newspaper in the land had followed Pa's trial. The name Revel had become a byword for dishonor and shame. Hettie could stop the newspapers at Lilycombe but she couldn't stop the millions of copies that arrived in shops up and down the country. During the months that followed the trial, Wolfie came, gradually, to understand the risk that Pa had taken on behalf of his men, the darkness of the shadow under which they'd now live, the burden of the name they carried.

The hills changed from brown to gold, the river parsley yellowing and straggling in the swollen currents.

Dodo, Wolfie, and Hettie got off the train and joined the surge of fairgoers, horses, ponies, and sheep towards the grey little village of Bampton.

Fifty or so ponies stampeded, wild, wide-eyed and terrified, up the single, purposeful street, between stolid houses and boarded shop fronts. Rounded up yesterday and branded, brood mares and stallions were returned to the moor, only the foals being brought to Bampton for selling.

All year Dodo had watched the silent heartbreak of her friend and teacher—each month, two, three, four more gone from the herd. Yet no one had seen anyone or anything, no one knew how or when they went. "It'd be someone that knows them," Father Lamb had said. "They're wild as snakes. Whoever it is knows these animals, really knows them." It'd been Samuel's suggestion that they go to Bampton and see if they were being sold there. The price of ponies and horses had gone up and up with the war, he'd said.

There was a wild tramp and thud of hoof on cobble as the ponies were corralled into sale pens, a separate pen for each herd, each pen labelled with the hill to which the herd was hefted. Caught up in the tightening crowd, Hettie and the children pushed and were pushed towards a pen.

Hettie examined each stamping, snorting herd, each time shaking her head and moving on. Bidding had started, brisk and raucous. Farmers and dealers shouted advice. Somewhere a pen was broken, the crowd shrieking. A pony whinnied and broke free from the ring attendant, wheeled away from the crowd, and burst into a tailor's shop. Over the noise, the bidding continued.

"Ten-Four . . . ten-four, ten-five?"

"Ten-five."

"Ten-six."

"Thank you, ten-six—going—going . . ." The hammer came down. "Gone."

It began to drizzle. They moved on, past ponies, more ponies, parsons, farmers, gentry.

"Are they all stolen?" whispered Wolfie, distracted by a pair of bare-fist boxers outside a pub.

"Shh," said Dodo.

"It's surely a great day for thieves and for rustlers," said Hettie, "but I don't see anything of mine here."

The drizzle thickened and they returned, none the wiser, by train to Dulverton, in a carriage loud with singing and livestock.

"Who could be taking them?" whispered Dodo.

"I don't know, Dodo, I just don't know."

At Dulverton they climbed into Hettie's trap. They wound up and out of the deep wooded valley, straight into the rays of the sinking sun, the sedge glowing fierce gold, flaming copper leaves above, a drift of gold on the lane. Hettie halted Scout. Against the skyline a herd of red deer, twenty perhaps, moved in silhouette, black against the orange sky.

"Look." She took Wolfie's hand. "As wild today as they've ever been. Like the ponies—here since William the Conqueror."

With tears in her eyes, she urged Scout on.

As they took the lane to Lilycombe they saw, on the corner, a tall figure, an unlit lamp in one hand, a brace of rabbit in the other. Wolfie waved. As Ned waved back, Hettie said, "Two thousand rabbits a day, did you know that—three tons of them are loaded just at Dulverton. Tuppence a rabbit they pay . . . It'll be a struggle for Ned to keep hold of that farm . . . he never wanted to take it on . . ."

Chapter Twenty-Two

Last week the mail had brought a letter from Pa. Vickers was alive but in a prisoner of war camp. Only if there were an exchange of prisoners and Vickers amongst them, would he be free to speak and testify in Pa's favor. Though there could not yet be an appeal, at least they knew, for certain now, that there was at least one other man living who knew the truth. Pa had not yet been moved from Wormwood Scrubs.

Wolfie kept Hero in a perpetual state of gleaming readiness in case Pa should suddenly be released. Father Lamb, sitting by his window, watched the boy run out to check the mail basket, then wander out into the garden, disconsolate. He saw the grey horse canter up and Wolfie sink his head against the dappled neck, twisting his hands into the long mane.

Dodo noticed that Father Lamb now sat at that window for his coffee, where once he'd always stood. Dreadnought's watchful head was now level with his master's shoulder. She turned, too, to watch Wolfie.

"That little boy's big heart will break if we don't have some good news soon," said Hettie.

"Why don't they at least send Pa to the mines?" asked Dodo. "He'd be happier there."

"It's probably only because of the difficulty of getting anything done in wartime conditions."

Father Lamb turned to his daughter. "Hettie, Hettie! Is it not race day today? Is it not today that Drew comes to do the judging? I should like to see my old friend. We could ride over there. Besides, Drew's a keen appreciator of horseflesh and he could look over that beast of young Wolfgang's."

Hettie watched him anxiously. "You should rest, Father."

Father Lamb took no notice. "You know, Hettie, the boy's got something special there—you can see the build of the horse now, the make of him . . . besides, the races would cheer us all up."

On the road to Comer's Gate, the sky opened and the sun broke through. Horses and ponies of all shapes and sizes converged in cheerful droves at the gate to a field that skirted the far side of the common. There they left the cart, tethered the horses, and wound their way between carts, farmers, dogs, and children towards striped sunlit tents, flags, and coconut shies.

Hettie and her father went first to the ale tent in search of Drew, then to the judging box. Dodo and Wolfie wriggled through the crowd to the edge of a makeshift grass track, where farmers, wives, and children sat on straw bales, watching and cheering. Among them were Mary Jervis and her husband.

Dodo stiffened. "Everybody's here today," she whispered.

The two drew closer together, wary and guarded.

A dark clot of horses was approaching, the crowd tensing and quieting. The field, all bone and muscle, flashed past, flanks steaming, turf flying, mud splattering onlookers.

"Hero would like to race one day," announced Wolfie.

"Wolfie, Hero has never run a race." Dodo bent her head and read from her program: "Hunters. Fifteen hands and over."

A hurdle race was to be next. Father Lamb, his hands behind his back, spied Dodo and Wolfie by the rope. Accompanied by a shorter, stouter man—his friend Drew—he made his way towards them. Dodo, seeing Father Lamb from a distance in a crowd, noticed for the first time his frailty, the pallor of his skin.

"Dodo." Wolfie put his hand on her arm. "Behind you!" he hissed urgently.

She turned. The three Causey girls, garishly dressed, stood together. Dodo backed away. The Causey girls stared and whispered behind their hands.

" 'Ee ran away," Chrissie said loudly. "Their father ran away an' now 'ee's in jail for it. That's why she's the teacher's favorite."

Dodo's cheeks burned.

"An' 'ee's lucky just to be in jail, my mum says. She says shootin' in't good enough . . ."

Wolfie stepped forward and shouted, fists clenched, eyes blazing. "He isn't—he's not—"

"Wolfgang." Father Lamb put a hand on his shoulder and turned him around. "Dodo, meet my old friend Drew."

"I knew your father," said Drew.

Wolfie's eyes glittered, still on his guard. Dodo hung her head.

"Pa's got a witness, one day there's going to be—" began Wolfie.

"I saw him. I was there, I saw him ride at Moreuil Wood."

Wolfie leaped forward.

"I saw him lead that squadron into the firing line," Drew continued, taking Wolfie's hands. "He had a fine grey that day. Fine *and* brave. Together they rode into the fire of five artillery companies, *five* of them. Never seen anything like it. Never will again."

"I've got a grey . . ."

"So I've heard. Would you mind if I took a look at him?"

They made their way to the edge of the field, where the horses grazed. Hero's head rose at Wolfie's whistle. Drew halted at a distance and surveyed Hero in silence. Wolfie waited, breath held.

"There's nothing on earth like a good horse, Wolf-gang," Drew said eventually, placing an arm round Wolfie's shoulders. "Now, you'd make my day if I could see that horse run." He picked up his list, and turned to Dodo. "Will you give permission for your brother to race? What do you think he should do? The Maiden—the Novice Stakes?"

"He'd like to race but he doesn't know what racing is," said Wolfie. "He doesn't go in circles, he goes in straight lines, because he's a charger."

"Well, let's show him about circles too. Let's try him in the Maiden Stakes."

Dodo began to remonstrate, but Drew was adding Wolfie to his list, leading him to the entry stand to collect a number.

"I'm putting a pound on you. I'm in London next week so I could get the winnings to your father . . . What do you say? It's just three laps, all on the flat." Drew checked his watch. "You've got ten minutes."

Drew took Father Lamb's arm and together they walked towards the judging stand.

Dodo, fingers trembling, tightened the girth for Wolfie, shortened his stirrups two stops.

Wolfie stood beside her, saying urgently, "He knows Pa, Dodo, he knows Pa and he saw him." Joy shone on Wolfie's face but as they walked away, leading Hero towards the roped enclosure, he grew hesitant. Ten or eleven horses had gathered for the Maiden Stakes, all sorts and sizes, shapes and colors. None wore silks or rugs. Like Hero they'd been brought here straight from the field, their manes and tails unkempt and loose. The riders were gentlemen farmers, or hunt staff or farm hands, some just boys, though none so young as Wolfie.

"I'm a bit scared," said Wolfie. Seeing a ripple of heads turn towards him, he added, "People are pointing at me."

"That's because you look rather small, Wolfie. Even your number placard's bigger than you are."

"I am *quite* small," said Wolfie.

"Keep him under control and stay on."

"He's going to see Pa—he'll tell him about Hero . . . ," began Wolfie.

"Just stay on, Wolfie, please JUST STAY ON."

Father Lamb followed Wolfie and Hero to the enclosure. Dodo unhooked the entrance rope and Wolfie stepped forward. Hero stopped dead, his tail lifted, and he snorted. His flanks began to quiver and his nostrils to flare.

"He's too excited," Wolfie whispered.

Father Lamb slapped Hero's rump and pushed him in, then gave Wolfie a leg up. Two riders were already leaving the paddock, still more were coming in. Hero stood out, silvery white against so many bays and chestnuts.

"I've got a shilling on you too," said Father Lamb.

"My heart is a bit wobbly," whispered Wolfie.

"Those that have no fear have no courage. Courage is the mastery of fear, not the absence of it, Wolfie," answered Father Lamb.

". . . And I have butterflies."

There were no riders left in the paddock now but Wolfie and Hero. Father Lamb rubbed Hero's nose.

"Get your butterflies in formation, Wolfie, get them into line . . . Don't let that horse go, don't let him *really* go, till you're ready. Then just keep going."

Drew's voice came over the loudspeaker.

"You have only thirty seconds to go, gentlemen . . . That's Drake Causey leaving the paddock now on Tinker, a smart sort of horse, bred up-country. That's Number Twelve. Behind Tinker, the youngest entrant, Wolfie Revel on the dapple grey at Number Five. A good-looking two-year-old, nice clean limbs, but both horse and jockey are untested on the flat. Behind him's Number Seven, the Master of the Devon and Somerset Staghounds. A fine rider there on Legacy. Legacy can hunt but can he race? . . . Twelve horses all in all for the Maiden Stakes."

Wolfie, with a parting glance at Dodo, followed the horses out to the starting line. Amidst so many older riders, he looked as incidental on the tall grey horse as though someone had left him there by accident. The riders were taking their place at the tape.

Hero was wary. Wolfie urged him on, coaxing him up to the tape. Hero pulled away, his ears flat back.

"I can't watch. Under no circumstances can I watch," whispered Dodo to Hettie.

Suddenly Hero spun round, almost unseating Wolfie, and was now facing the wrong way. He spun round again.

"They're under starters orders . . ."

The gun went.

"And they're off!"

The horses streamed away in a packed mass. Wolfie and Hero were left at the start line.

"Number One is ahead of the pack, behind him Seven and Twelve, neck and neck . . . It's a slow start for Number Five, who hasn't decided if he's going or not going."

Eagle-eyed, Hero watched and assessed. He began to paw the ground. Wolfie waited, watching Hero's ears, reading them like a book. Then Hero's muscles tensed. He raised his head. He raised his head higher, tall and majestic. His ears went forward, understanding, beginning to shiver with interest and excitement.

Wolfie bent and whispered, "Shall we go?"

Hero's ears flickered back, then pricked forward. Wolfie pressed his knees, loosed his rein, and whistled the first notes of the cavalry charge. Hero reared for joy, for joy and for good health and for the soft mown turf, then shot like a bullet from a gun down the track.

"Stay on, Wolfie, please just stay on," breathed Dodo. Wolfie didn't ride forward as the others did, but sat atop carelessly, as though he might at any minute fall. He felt Hero beneath him, smooth and steely and expert, smiled and loosed the rein a little more.

The main body of horses was streaming up the hill, now turning, now racing in silhouette along the skyline. Wolfie turned his head a little and saw them. Smiling, he whistled again, pressed with his knees. Hero moved effortlessly into a faster gallop. Wolfie pressed harder. Thrilled at his own gathering speed, Hero surged forward, ears leveled with the wind, finding unexplored power in himself, running faster now than he'd ever run. Wolfie's nerves melted. He closed his eyes and laughed—it was like riding a cloud or a shooting star.

They were approaching the judging stand, but still a long way behind the field. He saw the grey mane rising and falling and he breathed in and out, in with Hero, out with Hero, hearing in his own ears the roaring of the wind, the thunder of blood and hoof.

Dodo covered her face with her hands. Hettie nudged her and she separated her fingers a fraction. She saw clods of flying turf, opened her fingers a fraction more, saw the glittering eye and reaching neck.

"Number Five's young but he's fast. Look at the energy of him, the ambition of him—but he's a long way behind . . . If he's rideable at three, what'll he be as a five-year-old . . . ?"

The field was curving, more strung out now, onto the leftward, downward slope.

"Up at the front's Number One, Four's closing in on the inside, a promising young chestnut—they've still the third lap to go . . ."

"He's making time on them, Dodo," whispered Hettie.

"Something's happening at the back, Five's coming up on the outside, he's making time, he's catching the rump of the race. Look at that—he's past Four—making time on One—they're neck and neck . . . see the fierce youth of Number Five, both horse and rider . . ."

The fields were a blur, Hero's hoofs didn't touch the earth, the ground spun beneath them, insubstantial as a toy globe, they were suspended above the turf, they belonged to the sky, to the tattered gold-trimmed clouds.

"A feather—or a breeze—might knock that child off . . . We're into the third and final lap . . ."

Wolfie leaned low over the straining neck and whispered, "For Pa—Hero, let's go." He stayed low, his hands stretched forward, breathing with Hero, in with him, out with him, becoming part of the flow of the horse.

"The young grey's coming up on the inside—Number Five's on the inside, he's found a gap—he's coming up fast, he's passing them! Have you ever seen anything like it here at Comer's Gate? He's a streak of light—he's neck and neck with Seven. We're into the final furlong and Number Five—there's fire in him— he's a head ahead, he's a length ahead, he's found another gear, he's got another speed he didn't know he had! He's leading the field, he's leaving the field behind . . . He's left it behind—they're on the home straight and he's found he's got wings—he's outlasted, outstrided, outpaced all others . . . This horse didn't know he could run, and now he's running as though he's been doing it all his life . . ."

The crowd broke into a roar. Wolfie was laughing, tears streaming from his eyes. He and Hero were the sun and the wind and the sky.

"He's past the finish! What a horse—the courage of him! What a race! It's Number Five, young Revel on the dappled grey . . ."

Dodo saw her brother atop the sweat-streaked horse, the handsome grey head framed by the dark, loose mane, the tail a streaming banner, and tears sparkled on her cheeks. Wolfie braced his reins and pulled, slowing Hero up, bringing him back to a canter, now turning and trotting back to Dodo, waving, careless, the reins loose.

"A run to make a father's heart burst with pride—the courage of the Victoria Cross runs in this boy's veins, the mettle of it's in his marrow. His father led the last great cavalry charge the world'll ever see—was awarded the highest honor this country can bestow, and—now this! What a horse—Have you ever seen such a thing? What a horse, what symmetry, strength, grace! What a horse! And young Revel on him, the spirit of his father . . ."

He'd said it—a man who'd been there at the time had said it, in front of everyone—*"The courage of the Victoria Cross"*—here to the sun, to the stripy tents and golden clouds, to the purple hills and coconut shies, to schoolmates and to neighbors.

"And now the lap of honor . . . Behind him follow the Hunt staff, the hounds—Look at him, a horse

with stamina, with speed, with grace—a horse that'll be the envy of all England . . ."

As the hounds bayed and the bugle sounded and the crowd roared, Hero halted beside Dodo, snorting and heaving and steaming, nostrils wide and pink. Wolfie whispered, "Will you tell Pa, Dodo? Will you tell him everything?"

To the baying of the hounds and the sounding of the bugle and the cheering of the crowds, Wolfie and Hero rode the lap of honor. Father Lamb smiled at his daughter and winked. She took his arm and he leaned against her as they watched.

Chapter Twenty-Three

After the race Pa had written to Wolfie that the fame of Hero had reached even the darkest corner of London, and that Pa sat purring like a cat in the sun with the pride of it all. Pa thought that Wolfie must have breathed with Hero, in with him and out with him, so that they were one.

The winter that followed was cold and slow, March long and bitter. When April came it was wet and grey.

Antiaircraft batteries, artillery ranges, and search light positions were established on the open ground of the hills. The moor itself became a training ground for infantry and artillery. The noise of gunfire, shells, and mortar, became, for a while, a constant background that spring. The village filled with troops, British first, then American. Rumblings filled the valley, echoing and growing as convoys of monstrous tanks crawled across the old pack bridge. The old houses, smaller than the giant tanks, seemed to tremble with fear to see such things.

"Fifteen troop trains a day," said Father Lamb wistfully. "Each one with a thousand troops."

Stacks of ammunition stood outside the Village Stores. Blocks of gelignite piled up on roadsides like pats of margarine. Antiaircraft shells, hand grenades, dynamite, and mortars gathered on the roadsides. American jeeps burned and screeched down the narrow lanes. DUKW vehicles arrived, strange mongrels, armored cars crossed with boats. GIs sauntered through the villages in soft rubber-soled shoes, hands in their pockets, chewing gum, smiling, singing, lavish with tinned peaches, "candy," and cigarettes.

In the kitchen at Lilycombe, Wolfie looked over the Common, the brown moor beyond, a landscape as unwarlike as he could conceive. Father Lamb stood at his side, listened to the rumblings of the tanks through the open window, and said, "Twenty thousand troops up here, they say, and half of them American."

"Are we going to invade soon?"

"No. Not soon, not unless it stops raining."

Wolfie sat at the table and wrote to Pa.

Dear Pa,

I am glad you will appeal soon. Hero is bored because it keeps raining and the ground is too wet to ride.

The Americans are here. They put antlers on their jeeps. They give us toffee apples and oranges. They chew gum.

Love, Wolfie

PS The end of the war is going to start from here. Eisenhower is in the pub again today. His train has a cinema in it. There is lots of gelignite. There are tanks in the playing field at school. Father Lamb says the Americans feed their horses candyfloss and run their tanks on Coca-Cola. He says they are waiting for it to stop raining. I think something is going to happen soon.

Dodo, in secret, wrote a short note along the bottom of his letter before sealing the envelope:

Dear Pa,

Wolfie talks of nothing else but Hero and will never be quiet till you see him. It is a great strain.
    I hope Vickers will be exchanged so you have a witness and can make an appeal.

Love, Dodo

PS It is true that Eisenhower is here. He likes riding and he likes the Royal Oak.

Chapter Twenty-Four

The weather grew wetter and wetter, Hero more fretful and bored. By May it seemed the country was running with water. Meanwhile, almost on the doorstep of Lilycombe, General Eisenhower gathered the largest ever amphibian force. Piles of ammunition grew in fields among the bluebells. Tanks and jeeps waited in woods, camouflaged with netting and foliage. More tanks arrived, more troops, more jeeps, more lorries.

Still Eisenhower waited. Still the whole country waited.

Every morning Wolfie asked the same question.

"Will it be today?"

"Look." Father Lamb was peering at the map, Dreadnought at his side, looking up too. Dreadnought noticed no one else but Father Lamb, did everything that Father Lamb did. "Where d'you think we'll land?" He ran his fingers along the French coast. "We might pretend to go to Calais, then quietly go somewhere else. And how'll we land?" He tapped his fingers on the map. "Where can we land two and a half thousand vehicles in a single day?" He turned and said, "Wolfie, it's going to be like nothing the world's ever seen before—it's the most critical operation of the war, Eisenhower's got to get it right the first time, got to get the right moment . . . he needs a calm crossing."

He took his coffee to the table, sat down, and drank, then said, "That man must be beside himself with fear that it could all go wrong. As he sits down there, in the Royal Oak, he must fear that this could be another Somme, another Gallipoli."

Pa wrote that there was to be a second exchange of prisoners, that perhaps Major Vickers might be among them. Free then at last to talk, he'd say what had happened. Pa's story would at last be proven, and he could then appeal and clear his name. For Wolfie, he'd added an extra note:

Always make a horse feel secure. Hero must know that you'll never let him down. They have long memories. A horse has a very long memory. You must never, never break trust with a horse, Wolfie.

The weather stayed bad. The country waited, tense as a coiled spring. On Sunday Samuel told Hettie that Monday and Tuesday would be fine, that there'd be a storm today, but the following days would be clear.

Samuel always knew when to take sheep off a hill, when to harvest, when to sow.

On Sunday the fields and roadsides and woods began to empty of ammunition and vehicles. By Monday, the lanes and villages were as empty as if the whole country had gone across the Channel to settle with Hitler. There were no tanks in the playing field at school. That night, as the children wished him good night, Father Lamb said, "Churchill will be a worried man tonight. At least three hundred thousand men will cross that Channel tomorrow. By the time the country wakes, what will've happened? Will twenty thousand men be dead? Will the Channel run with blood?"

"Father . . . ," interrupted Hettie, shocked.

"You must pray for them," said Father Lamb.

At eight the next morning, the BBC bulletin announced that paratroopers had landed in northern France. Wolfie bought a Red Cross flag at the crossroads and dropped a penny in the tin. All the way to school Wolfie chanted Eisenhower's words: *"The eyes of the world are upon you. The hopes and prayers of liberty-loving people everywhere march with you . . ."*

At nine forty-five, on the wireless in the schoolroom, Wolfie heard Eisenhower call to the Allies in France, Belgium, and Holland, "Be patient, be patient, we are coming."

* * *

At ten o'clock the D-Day landings were announced. They heard cheers in the streets, people singing "Land of Hope and Glory." In the village that evening, Father Lamb gave an impromptu service of thanksgiving, the church filled to overflowing, tears on everyone's faces.

Dodo and Wolfie were quiet, holding hands, thinking of Pa, alone in a military jail.

Chapter Twenty-Five

After the Normandy landings, the summer had greyed and sagged. Rationing had taken a tighter grip. Germany was firing sinister, pilotless bombs on London.

There'd been no good news from London. Pa was still waiting to hear if Vickers was to be among the prisoners exchanged, still waiting to be moved to the mines. Wolfie and Dodo had picnicked at Pennywater with the ponies. Their mood was subdued and melancholy and when the sky grew thick and woolly, they mounted their horses and headed for home. The first fat round drops of rain began to fall. The sky grew violet. Gunmetal clouds rolled and heaved in monstrous towers.

They rose from the wooded droveway onto the brow of the hill, and into a solid wall of wind and rain. Over the hill beyond Lilycombe, clouds reared, menacing as wild animals against the ribboned sky. Wind battered the heather, bending and shaking the rush, nerving them homeward. They kicked onward.

A summer gale was gathering. Rain billowed like smoke.

"Hurry, Wolfie!" called Dodo, alarmed by the sudden transformation of the day, by the driving rain, the rearing, bucking wind. Finally they reached the lane and took the shortcut home.

As they reached Lilycombe, there was a savage crash, a heart-stopping flash, the yard brilliant with white light. The door of the farm was flung open and Hettie ran out, two oilskins in her hand.

"Father—the lines are down—the cables down—no telephone—will you go for me—to the doctor—fetch the doctor . . ."

Dodo nodded. They fumbled with the coats, the sleeves of them spinning and flapping in the wind, and turned their unwilling horses out of the yard down towards the river and the next village.

Again they rode into the guttering, streaming wind, unnerved by the crying, the raging of the river, the straining and the creaking of the trees. Shivering and streaming with water, they arrived at the little house beside the Post Office.

"It's wind to blow the sea onto the land," said Doctor John doubtfully, unlatching his stable door.

When they made their way back, the river had swollen to a torrent, the narrow track high above it slipping and sliding beneath their hoofs. The wind screamed in their ears, caught up a myriad of hectic, swirling leaves around their feet. Somewhere in the whirling night there was a savage crash, a tree pulled mercilessly from its socket.

Lovely Lilycombe was a beacon of amber light and warmth. Hettie hadn't closed the curtains, but she had managed to lift her father, to carry him from where he'd fallen, to a makeshift bed on a sofa by the fire. At his master's side, Dreadnought whimpered softly.

Later, the children were sent to bed while the doctor and Hettie spoke quietly, her face drawn and grey. Outside the wind whined around Lilycombe like a coven of witches. The old windows rattled, the old house creaked like a boat on a stormy sea.

By morning the doctor had left and the crisis had passed. Father Lamb had recovered his speech and his movement, was cross with himself to have troubled the doctor and his horse to come out on such a night.

Chapter Twenty-Six

The wind had dropped as suddenly as it had arisen but there'd been steady rain for three days. On the last day of the holidays the rain stopped and they woke to opaque mist, the sun white and mysterious as a moon.

Hettie rushed into their room, hugged the sleepy Wolfie, and hurried the children downstairs.

"We've had a letter—you've a letter waiting . . ."

On the breakfast table, propped up against a green vase of yellow gorse, stood an envelope from Pa. Father Lamb sat in a chair by the church window, a blanket round his shoulders, his head drooping. Dodo and Wolfie read the letter together.

My dearest Dodo, dearest Wolfie,

Box, my dear Sergeant Box, companion of both wars, survived—he got himself out of that barn—escaped the SS—and was later taken prisoner, wounded, and placed in a German hospital. He's been sent home now, as medically unfit. He wrote to me that he had lost his legs, that he's home, but hospitalized. He says, God bless him, that when he's well, he'll fight with every last drop of his blood to clear my name.

I will appeal, when Box is well enough, but still hope, in the meantime, that they'll finally send me to the mines.

Toodleoo, Pa

"They will let him out," said Wolfie. "If Pa appeals they will let him out."

"Yes and his name would be cleared. You must celebrate for him," said Hettie. "It'll be sunny and I've prepared you a picnic."

"Will you come, will you and Father Lamb come?" whispered Dodo.

"No." She smiled bravely. "I'll stay with Father. Doctor John's back later today and I'd be happier staying." She added a flask of lemonade to the basket, "Go to Hoar Oak, it will be beautiful up there today."

"Shall I stay with you?' asked Dodo.

"No, Father must rest and I must be here when Doctor John comes. But you must go and relish this God-given day."

In the yard she buckled Pa's bag and strapped that

and Wolfie's bugle to Hero's saddle. "Check the ponies on your way out and steer clear of the rivers," she said to Dodo. "They're high and the ground's wet after so much rain."

Pennywater was swollen, the old withy severed from its roots, but the ponies stood in a circle of sunlight close by, grazing peacefully on the fresh wet grass.

They left the rutted, leaf-strewn lane for the hill. On top the light was sharp as a blade, everything washed clean. Hero broke into a canter on the soft ground.

"It's like riding through a painting," said Dodo.

Wolfie didn't answer but laughed happily, leaning forward, arms draped down over the dappled neck, cheek to Hero's mane.

They jumped the glimmering runnels between the reeds, laughing and whooping. Racing across the heather, they dodged the sheep that clustered like so many daisies amidst the pink. On they went, whooping and laughing, their chests big with hope. *Box would tell the truth, Box would clear Pa's name.*

Ahead lay the cliffs and the sea. To the left lay the valley known as Hoar Oak Water.

At Sheepwash they dropped down, off the hill and out of the wind. Scout was arthritic and careful, seeking the soft side of the bony deer path; behind her, Hero was springy and rhythmic and easy. Beneath them, amber water looped and turned and sung its way over rosy shale. *Hoar Oak Water.* Dodo liked to imagine that their mother had painted here, that she used to come to this spot.

The warmth of the day was cupped in the narrow valley, like breath in a palm. They went on, taking the narrower cleave that opened onto Hoar Oak Water. Long Chains Coombe was a cleave of fairy-tale loveliness, the swollen stream a sparkling filigree of amber and silver. They let the horses drink, then crossed the water and loosely tethered them where the bank was soft and flat, to an old alder.

Wolfie skimmed pebbles over the fleecy water. Dodo looked up at the treacherously steep hill on the other side of the water, then sighed and lay back on the turf. She listened to the mesmerizing muttering of the stream and, after a while, said, "Here it all seems far away and impossible—the war, Pa's case, the trial, his sentence . . ."

She began to peel a squished boiled egg. Wolfie turned his attention to a small stone, all encrusted with black and gold, yellow and white. He came back to the bank and reached for his magnifying glass.

"What do you see, Wolfie, when you look?" asked Dodo, watching him.

"Lichen," said Wolfie stoutly. "Lots of lichen."

Dodo took the glass. "I see," she said, "a fairy-tale garden, all pink and silver, a place where nothing horrid will ever happen."

"When Pa sees Hero it will be like a storybook," he answered, "and we can all live here with Hero."

"I like to imagine Ma was here, that she used to come and paint here," said Dodo.

Wolfie didn't answer.

"The ponies," said Dodo eventually. "I'm only scared now about the ponies."

"And Father Lamb," said Wolfie. "I am worried about Father Lamb too."

A damselfly whirred past, wings flashing like fragments of fire. Dodo picked up her charcoal and sketch pad, turning to the head of Long Chains Coombe, where three hills draped themselves and joined their ancient, pleated feet at the cradle of the glacial valley.

Wolfie unwrapped a sandwich. Shadow patterns of alder played on Hero's dappled coat. Hero flicked his tail and tossed his head, annoyed at the horseflies that had come out with the sun. Alarmed to discover so much green in his sandwich, Wolfie picked out trails of watercress for him. Hero ate from Wolfie's hand, lifting and turning his head as he chomped, to the hill where the moor rush billowed like the crest of a wave.

The day ripened and hummed, gilding the westward wave of rush. Wolfie rolled up his trousers and began to build a dam, in the same spot as he'd built one last time they'd been here. Dodo abandoned her charcoal, lay back, and dozed.

* * *

The sun abandoned the valley. Wolfie was still at his dam when Dodo was woken by a fresh breeze. She shivered. The sky was greying, the sparkle of the day gone. Scout was fretting at her rope. Ready to go home, Dodo thought, watching her snort and paw the ground.

Scout pulled free, snapping the branch that tethered her, tangling her rope. She reared, trying to free herself, pounding the soft grass, rearing again, nostrils flaring, eyes wide.

"Scout's loose!" Dodo called. "Help me, Wolfie."

Wolfie, astride two stepping-stones, heard only the pealing of the water but he saw Dodo run barefoot along the bank, dodging dwarf thistles. With a firm hand on Scout's neck, Dodo managed to disentangle the halter but Scout was breathing heavily, light and wary on her forelegs.

"Shh, it's all right." Dodo heard the quaver in her own voice. Usually so stout and steady, Scout seemed suddenly primeval and the fear in her was unsettling and contagious. Dodo glanced at Hero but the young grey horse was still, his deep gaze towards the homeward, eastward ridge of moor grass. Dodo followed his eyes and saw the sinister glow of it, fire-red as if burnished by a desert sun.

Scout whipped round, shrieking, tearing the rope through Dodo's hands, knocking her to the ground. Then the mare wheeled round and charged towards Hero. She nudged his flank with the bone of her head, nudged again. Hero whinnied and pulled at his rope. Dodo, on the ground between them, saw, properly now, the crest of the Hoar Oak valley, orange-red, the whole horizon a ridge of flame. Fear leaped inside her like a wild thing.

"Quick, Wolfie—quick—fire—there's a fire!" she yelled.

Scout whinnied again, shoving Hero with her head.

"First bridle Hero," Dodo said to herself, "then Scout. She'll stay—she won't bolt without him."

With fumbling, panicky fingers, they bridled the horses.

"Hurry, Wolfie, HURRY!" Dodo screamed as Wolfie scrabbled at the girth, the terrified Hero pulling and dancing and throwing his head. "Don't let go, whatever you do, don't let him bolt," Dodo said to Wolfie. "It's OK, OK," she breathed to Scout, but she could hear the fear in her own voice.

Wolfie pulled Hero towards a rock from which to mount, but the horse threw his head, yanking the rope from his hands. Scrabbling for it, Wolfie called out to Dodo but his voice was lost in the rushing water, his horse wild and feral.

Dodo tethered Scout tightly to the withy and went to help. Scout squealed and struck at the tree. Hero reared and thrashed, wild-eyed with fear. He spun round, knocking Dodo to the ground. She cried out and doubled up in searing pain, knees to her chest, the wind taken out of her. Wolfie caught the rope and held the jigging, prancing horse.

"Get on—get on him," Dodo called from the ground. She forced herself to stand and staggered over, biting her lip in pain, holding out her left arm for the rope. "Just get *on*," she pleaded.

Wolfie looked at her in horror, her right arm hanging limp, her eyes starred with silent, valiant tears.

"Quick as you can," she said, her voice trembling, holding Hero with her left arm, her left hand pushing deep into the soft spot of his neck to control him. Wolfie stood on his stone and scrambled on.

Dodo clutched her right arm to her chest. She looked up and scanned the tops of the hills. The eastward, homeward stretch of heather was all orange flame. The Hoar Oak ridge was all orange flame, the southward ridge above Long Chains Coombe was orange flame. To the north lay the sea cliffs, cliffs higher than Dover, that plunged vertically to the sea. To the west lay the Chains. The fire had started perhaps near Sheepwash, thought Dodo, and it had a good eastward wind behind it. Dodo cast around. That slope to the south was too steep for the horses, they must follow the valley to the west. She took her coat and tied, one-handed, a knot in the sleeves, then placed it round her neck. Easing the bad arm in, she stumbled over to Scout.

A stag, sudden and prehistoric, was flying up the cleave towards them, leaping along the far side of the water towards the head of the valley. A dark knot of ponies raced, huddled and tight, along the northward ridge towards the west and the Chains. Follow the animals, Dodo calculated, follow the stag.

She'd have only seconds to mount. Once she'd unclipped Scout's rope she'd bolt.

Dodo stepped up onto a hump beside Scout. She put one foot in the stirrup in readiness. Scout tossed her head and pawed the ground. Dodo pulled herself up with her good arm and lent forward to unclip the halter but Scout reared and tore herself free, jumping to one side in a sudden cat leap, tangling Dodo in the low branches of the withy. Dodo doubled over her neck, searching for the other stirrup, as Scout plunged down to the stream, splashed and slipped across the stones, then leaped up the bank on the far side, Dodo still fighting to stay on.

When she could, she turned to check where Wolfie was. He was behind, Hero's muzzle to Scout's tail. Scout was careering towards a zigzagging track at the head of the cleave, a track known as Postman's Path, the same path the stag had taken. Fitful and panicky with fear, Scout stumbled and staggered up the steep, crumbling shillet.

As they neared the top, a warm, dry wind whipped their shirts, whipped the horses' manes. The fire was spreading, the strong wind from the east, the cliffs to the north, and the impassable slope to the south. They would be forced westward with the stag and the ponies. Scout staggered onto the ridge, her chest heaving.

Dodo cast around, feeling the fierce, dry rush of the fire, her single hand trembling on the reins. A sea of flame stretched to the eastward, homeward horizon, and southward. Hero whinnied and pranced, wide-eyed and whirling, smelling the fire.

Scout, recovering from the hill, began to jig and pirouette like a circus horse, clockwise then anticlockwise. Dodo saw the hunger of the fire, the leaping tongues and swirling sparks. Gulls wheeled hectic circles overhead, like confetti in a storm.

"It's spreading," she whispered, looking to the path they'd come, across the flaming homeward sky, turning to the northward cliffs and then to the country they didn't know, the Chains. "The Chains is our only hope," she said. "The ground there's wet, rushy . . ."

Chapter Twenty-Seven

Scout, too, had decided to head for the Chains.

"Stay close!" yelled Dodo as they rode towards the rush. "Stay with me, Wolfie."

Rush stood in drifts waist high, for as far as she could see, each blade of it glinting with the sinister amber of the fire. The ground would be hard going, all tall tussocks and sudden peaty holes.

Dodo's reins were loose now over the saddle, her right arm held close to her chest by her left, only her legs free to grip with. Scout staggered and lurched, making heavy weather of the difficult ground. She stumbled and plummeted into a yielding, treacherous pocket of mossy wet. She paused, her flanks heaving, her forelegs mired. Thrown forward over Scout's neck, hugging her arm to her chest in pain, Dodo waited for Scout to regain her footing.

The ground was threaded with broken streams and pools of standing water that held the sky like fragments of bloodied glass. Dodo closed her eyes and tried to blot out the pain in her arm and shoulder, clenched her muscles to squeeze out the quaking of her legs.

"*Stick to the heather,*" Hettie had always said. "*Heather likes to be dry*"—but they'd had no choice.

A marsh bird rose and whirled away, startled.

Dodo whispered Scout on. Scout squealed but didn't move. Dodo kicked her, the movement in her legs sending a bolt of pain down her arm, but Scout only shrieked and tossed her head. Again Dodo kicked, again and again. Scout lowered her head and soldiered on, sloshing, lurching, sinking to her hocks at each step in black mud.

Dodo's arm burned, her chest burned. Her breath was panicky and jerky with fear. Scout's flanks heaved with exhaustion but she staggered on and on, then suddenly her left foreleg was deep into the soft liquid earth, sinking deeper and deeper, to her forearm. She paused, quivering, then wrenched it out, heaving with the effort of it, but now her left foreleg was sinking, sinking deeper and deeper into soft, liquid earth.

A trail of strange water plants clung to Scout's legs. A strange acid smell was released from the earth. Dodo choked and half retched on the stench of it. Sphagnum. They were in a sphagnum bog. That foreleg was in to the elbow. Dodo panicked and kicked again hard. Scout squealed. She was quivering and straining, trying to dislodge first one leg, then the other. She pulled but couldn't release them.

She started to wheeze, her nostrils pink and wide

with fear. With an immense and sudden effort, Scout reared, almost unseating Dodo, who clung with her left hand to her mane. Scout fell, plunging a little to the right, but she was sinking, forelegs falling, sinking deeper in, deeper and deeper in. Like a boat, she was listing in the mud, the left side of her deeper in than the right, mired now to the elbows, in sphagnum sponge.

"*Sphagnum lies over liquid peat.*" Hettie's words echoed in Dodo's head. There'd be nothing below them but liquid peat!

Scout whinnied, a shrill, gaunt warning.

Hero answered from behind.

"Get back, Wolfie!" Dodo yelled. "No—stay where you are—don't move." She was paralyzed by pain, nauseous with fear. *Sphagnum.* They were caught, trapped in a swaying pool of sphagnum. "Wolfie—hold him back—hold him—don't let him follow!" she screamed, half retching with the acid stench.

Minutes passed. She must wait for Scout to regain her strength; those forelegs were still quivering, the flanks still heaving. Dodo's ears droned with the humming of small flying things. She looked around again, searching for she knew not what. Fifteen feet or so away, there was rush. Rush and a stunted thicket of alder and sallow. Beyond the bog, the lonely empty miles of rush stretched away on all sides.

"*Rush doesn't care for the worst places,*" Hettie always said. "*It likes water but prefers her roots firmly anchored.*"

She must get Scout to that thicket. Only a short distance and the ground would be firm. Trembling like a leaf, she pleaded, "Please . . . please, Scout . . ." She kicked, kicked again. Pain shot up her arms, across her chest. Scout's neck heaved and swelled, her nostrils flared. She tried to move her forelegs, but they floundered, the mud rising above Dodo's stirrups, over her boots. Each attempt at movement was sending Scout's legs deeper in.

Tears streamed down Dodo's cheeks.

Hero pawed the ground, splashing, his neck straining forward. Dodo turned to Wolfie, saw all his strength pitted against his horse. She looked down at Scout's flanks, saw the mud line over the belly, and screamed, "She's in to her stifles! She's sinking—there's no bottom, Wolfie!"

"I can't hold him back, Dodo—I can't!" he answered.

Scout whinnied. Dodo heard the heart-stopping cry, heard the raw fear in its every note. Hero heard it and plunged forward, snatching the reins from Wolfie's hands.

Dodo turned and saw his grey legs flail and flounder, saw the spraying of the black mud, the terror in his eyes, saw Wolfie, frozen with fear, thrown forward over his neck.

"Oh God, oh God," she breathed, then shouted, "Stay on him—just stay on him—for God's sake, stay on!"

Hero pawed the ground, his forelegs struck the air. Wolfie recovered the reins, gripped a fistful of mane and jabbered, "Stay, Hero—stay—please don't move—don't move."

Dodo's body quaked, she couldn't get her legs, her arm, to do her bidding, the pain was spreading, her frame convulsed with fitful shivering. Get the saddle off, she thought, I've got to get the saddle off . . . I must get off, then get it off. She lifted her leg, yanked up the saddle flap, and fumbled with the girth. One buckle—the second—both buckles undone—now she must dismount. Slowly she leaned forward over the saddle, gently swung her leg over and slipped down, easing her trembling body into the dreadful mire. Holding Scout's mane, she pushed the saddle with her good arm, tipping it off and letting it fall.

Clinging to Scout, she ran a trembling hand along the ridge of Scout's neck, down her back, scratching gently where the saddle had been.

Hero cried out, a raw, shrill scream. Scout cried back, a low bark, mournful as an echo.

Dodo started. She ran her hand feverishly up and down Scout's shoulder . . . her withers, her neck. They were still, the trembling gone. She clutched at Scout's head, pulled at her mane.

"No—no—try—please try—Scout, try—try . . . no one on your back, no saddle . . ." She slapped at Scout's rump, slapped at her neck, drummed and drummed at it and pleaded.

"Dodo! Dodo!" Wolfie was calling.

Scout's head was dropping. Dodo screamed to her, slapped her again with her bare hands, but Scout's lids were drooping, her head dropping, she was surrendering, giving in, sedated by the treacherous tropical warmth of the bog.

"No—no no no no no, Scout—please . . . don't give in," Dodo pleaded.

Scout half opened her heavy lids. The loving amber eyes gazed out dozily, blinked, then closed. Dodo grabbed and pulled at her mane, crying to her, pulling at her head. She placed her hand beneath Scout's muzzle to lift her head but she herself had nothing to stand on, nothing to push against. If she tried to move her legs the slime was resistant and solid as sand, yet she was sinking deeper through it.

Scout's chin rested peacefully along the inky surface. Dodo saw that lovely head, the tender eyes, the golden mane, the golden ridge of her neck, she saw the black tide creeping, higher, inch by inch up the swell of her belly, and she clung to Scout, Scout, the faithful, tender companion of so many days, and she was nauseous with the horror of what was happening.

Somewhere, Wolfie was shouting, "Dodo, he can't move—he's not sinking—I don't think he's sinking but . . ."

Wolfie sounded far away and long ago. Dodo was hot and cold and quaking, one arm only with which to cling to Scout, and the slime was seeping down her shirt, seeping down her back, the warmth of it sinister and soupy.

The crest of Scout's neck stood in a ridge above the black, only her neck and her head were clear of the slime, but her muzzle was wide, as if smiling, her eyes closed.

"Dodo!" someone was screaming. "Please, Dodo, please come!"

The black tide was rising over the whiskery chin, over the mottled lips, seeping into the rosy nostrils. Dodo flicked away a small flying thing that had settled on the corner of Scout's eye, then she rested her head against Scout's cheekbone.

Somewhere someone was still screaming, somewhere a horse was shrieking, but they were muffled and blurred, still far away and long ago. Around Scout were strange yellow asphodels and sundews that Dodo hadn't seen before, entwined in the emerald moss, like unearthly jewels. She whispered and she stroked and she whispered and stroked until Scout's ear lay still, until all that was there were the last strands of Scout's forelock, floating like spun gold on the mire.

Wolfie screamed, screamed, and screamed again, but Dodo wasn't moving, wasn't answering, her right cheek and one arm lay outstretched on the surface of the peat, clutching at the air.

He must get Hero to her, he must save Dodo. He must lead his horse forward to the place where another horse had drowned.

"*Never break faith with a horse, Wolfie.*" Pa's words rattled in his head like knives. Tears slid down his cheeks, but he was kicking Hero with desperate, panicky jabs.

"Go on, Hero, go on," he yelled. "Go, go, go . . . DodoDodoDodoDodo!"

Still she didn't answer; that arm was sinking.

"Go on, go on, go on . . . ," he yelled again, kicking and jabbing with his heels.

Hero snorted. He lifted his head, his eyes blazed, and he plunged, flaying through the mud, stabbing at it, knees high, crying out as he went.

Four paces, only four, and they'd be at her side—not "paces": four rears, four plunges and they'd reach her. Wolfie kicked and screamed and kicked and screamed. The young horse reared and plunged, reared and plunged, reared and plunged.

"*Never break faith with a horse, Wolfie.*" Wolfie couldn't see for tears, for the horror and fear of it.

Wolfie pulled at the reins. Hero stopped, heaving, snorting, streaming, head high, legs testing the ground. There was solid ground beneath one hoof—beneath the right foreleg—on the side where Dodo was. There was solid ground. Wolfie leaned out, reached for her arm, and pulled, hands slipping and losing the slimy black of her sleeve, clutching at it again, grasping her hand, losing it, reaching, gripping, pulling the length of her arm, hand over hand, till he had her under the arm. He heaved her shoulder, her head against his knee. He turned her face towards him and screamed as he saw the closed eyes, slapped her cheeks, and cried, "Wakeupwakeupwakeupwakeup!"

Her eyes half opened, then closed. He dragged her, but the mud was squelching and sucking at her and it took all his strength to lift her an inch or two up, to pull her arm across the front of Hero's saddle.

"Still, Hero. Stay still, don't move, just stay." Wolfie's voice was whispery and panicked. Hero was adjusting his position, the left foreleg was carrying the weight of the three of them. "Still, Hero, stay still, don't move, don't move, just stay . . . ," Wolfie urged quietly. He slapped Dodo again, again and again, but her face was pale, her eyes closed and unmoving, her long hair in his hands turned to ropes of black all trailed with green. "Please . . . please . . . Someone come . . . someone come . . . ," he whispered.

But there was only the primeval, tractless waste, the glistening mire, the deafening humming of small flying things.

A dragonfly rested on Dodo's cheek, then whirred away, its wings flashing satanic green.

Wolfie whispered to Hero, he whispered to Dodo. He whispered and called, called and whispered to them both, till he had no breath, till it seemed that hours, that days perhaps had gone by.

A wild duck clattered up from a silver runnel, starting Wolfie. He must have slept. Soft, misty rain was falling, dusk and mist and bog all merging. Everything was water, the earth, the air, were all water. He yelped, jerky with fear, shaking Dodo, finding her shoulders rigid, her face cold and damp to his palm. He called out in fear—"Hero, HERO!"

The horse blinked, turned his head a fraction, and calmly shifted his weight. Dodo's hand was cold in Wolfie's, her forehead cold, but he felt the slow, steady pulse of her heart against his thigh.

"Dodo, DodoDodoDodo!" he yelled. "Wake up, wake up, wake up, wake up, wakeupwakeupwakeup."

But there was only the soundless silence, the air as still as if time were suspended. There was no sun, no sky, no dark, no distance, color or sound, only the black mire and the thickening grey-white air.

Wolfie's fingers fumbled for the warm withers, frantically stroking the hair and skin of the horse that was the only clear and solid thing in the disorientating white.

Some way away there was a movement, a shape, whiter than the surrounding white, slipping thinly in and out of the luminous whiteness, phantom-like.

His mind was playing tricks, the desolate white was worse than the black of night, everything dissolved, the hag line, the sunken alder, the brown hills, all blotted out.

"Help!" Wolfie called, but his voice was absorbed in the muffling whiteness as in a sponge.

A rustling made him leap from his skin, the

rustling of something unseeable in the weird ghost world. Wolfie shook Dodo, pulled at her hair. Hero lifted his head and snorted a belly-deep bark. Wolfie pulled again at Dodo's hair, shaking her, his hand falling on something metallic and cold. He grappled at the buckle, wretched and clumsy, yanking the bugle free. He blew, and blew again, but the sound was absorbed in the spongy white.

"HalloooooOOO!" came a voice.

"Help!" Wolfie called back.

There was movement somewhere, then the same voice closer now.

"Pinford, they're in Pinford. Or the Devil's Stable."

There was silence for a while. Then, nearer now, stood a brown shadow, bending and peering.

"Don't move."

Ned—that was Ned's voice.

"Ned!" Wolfie screamed. "Ned!" He was shaking from top to toe, his knees banging against the saddle roll. He saw a coil of rope over Ned's arm, the shape of a rifle under the other. "She won't wake up—Dodo—she won't wake up."

"Wait and don't move. 'As the horse got solid under him?"

"No . . . Yes—one foot, I think."

The figure turned.

"No! Don't go! Don't go!" yelled Wolfie.

"Wait an' I'll be back."

"Wake up, Dodo, wake up wakeupwakeup!" Wolfie pleaded.

An age seemed to pass. Hero's head was dropping. Tears of mist clung to the hairs of his coat. Wolfie was hoarse with whispering, he had no words left. Ned might never come back and his own head was sinking to Hero's neck, he and Dodo both clinging to Hero like drowning men to a crag.

Ned came with a plank. Leaving his coat and gun on the ground, he snapped off a stem of alder and slid the plank out from the hag line towards Hero. Wading out, he slid and pushed it farther, then crawled along it on all fours.

He saw Dodo's blue lips, took a flask from his pocket, and forced her mouth open, splashing whisky in. Her arms and legs jerked, her head jolted, and she spluttered, suddenly wide-eyed and shivering.

Dodo's sight focused. She saw Ned's white face, the red stain on the cheek, and she turned, searching wildly, reaching out her hand. "Wolfie? Wolfie?" she whispered. Her hand found his. "Wolfie, thank God, thank God."

Ned took her under the arms. She screamed out in pain, but he pulled her over to the plank.

"Broken," he said after a while. "Rib maybe. Collarbone. Arm." He smoothed the hair off her face, wiped the black off her cheeks, and smiled at her.

"Lots o' bits of you broken. Aye, an' you're lucky to get out. So much rain, there's bogs even where there's been none afore."

He crawled to the far end of the plank, then dragged it gently up onto the rush so Dodo could crawl off.

"Get the saddle off him. Get yourself onto the plank," he called to Wolfie, pushing the plank back out. "Then stay there."

The plank swung on the strange green suspension, each movement of Wolfie's as he struggled with the girth causing an echoing movement somewhere on the trampoline surface.

He looked up and saw the eyes that followed his every movement and he trembled before the fathoms of trust in them.

Dodo huddled, shivering on the rush.

Ned placed his feet on the end of the plank and said to Wolfie, "My weight's on it now, start moving towards me."

Wolfie looked at Hero, then turned back to Ned.

"No," he said, shaking his head, "No."

"Leave him. Won't make it—nothin' under him, no traction."

"He will . . . he will get out—he can—"

"No." Ned's voice was loud and angry. "Get yourself out. Now."

Dodo was crawling across the rush. Wolfie saw her reach for the rifle, stagger to her feet, one arm held to her chest, the other holding the trigger, no hand to steady the barrel of it. She raised the rifle at Ned.

When Ned turned and saw, he froze.

"Get him out. Get Hero out," said Dodo, her voice shaking, the barrel of the rifle wobbling.

Ned was silent for a few seconds, then, his eyes on Dodo, he shouted to Wolfie, " 'Oow long? 'Oow long's he been in there?"

"I don't know," he answered.

"Get him out," said Dodo.

" 'E's nothin' under him," Ned said, "nothin' to push off."

"He's not sinking," Wolfie said. "There's solid under him where two legs are, it's solid."

Ned thought for a minute, then said, "Put the gun down." Without turning to Dodo, he said to Wolfie, "Have you asked him to get out? Has he tried? Is he tired?"

"No, no, and no," answered Wolfie.

"Tell 'er to put the gun down," said Ned.

Dodo lowered the barrel. Ned bent to pick up the coil of rope and began to poke around in the alder for a long branch.

Halfway along the plank, Ned tested the depth with his stick. He bent, bent farther, then knelt, his arm submerged to the shoulder. "Ten foot maybe," he said. "Too deep."

Dodo raised the rifle. "What are you doing?" she said, pink rising in her cheeks. "What are you doing out here with a rope? With a rifle? It's not your land."

Ned, standing on an unsteady plank, in a bog, with a rifle raised at him, said nothing.

"Why did the fire get out of control? You weren't swaling, were you? Not now, not at this time of year?"

"Sent to find you I was," he answered, his eyes on the horse. "You were lucky it hit that grass. The rush here's thicker, doesn't burn like the other stuff. It's broken the path of the fire."

"Was it on purpose, Ned Jervis, that fire?"

Ned bent slowly, conscious of the rifle aimed at him. He crouched on the precarious plank and, after a few tries, managed to loop the rope around Hero's neck.

"Don't move," he said to Wolfie. "Stay where you are—steady as you can—or I go in. When I tell you, you ask him, just the once, shout an' lash together—good an' hard—*hard*, hard as you can. At the same time I pull."

Wolfie nodded.

"All depends on his character, on the spirit in him. Some give in, some don't. Depends on the fight in 'em."

"Hero will fight," said Wolfie, looking Ned in the eyes as he took the stick Ned held out.

Back on the rush, with the end of the rope in his hands, Ned nodded to Wolfie.

Wolfie rose and placed his legs apart, bracing himself. He looked at Hero. Hero's head turned and gazed back at the boy, his eyes luminous with love and trust. Wolfie breathed deeply, then he, who'd never, ever taken a whip to his horse, raised a stick high above his head. The dark almond eyes watched him and watched the stick.

"Hero, you've got to do it—got to get out . . . ," he whispered.

Wolfie took a deep breath and nodded to Ned. "Out. Get out!" he yelled and lashed. "Now! Out!"

Wolfie lashed again, yelled again, lashed again.

"Gerr'on," shouted Ned, and pulled.

Wolfie lashed again, tears streaming down his cheeks. "Come, Hero," he pleaded. "Now!" He raised the whip again.

Hero tensed, his nostrils flared, his neck arched, his spine arched, his neck was corded with swelling veins, his eyes blazing, and his forelegs were fighting free of the holding squelch—they were high and clear, doubled, like a jumping stag—he was swinging and falling—plunging down—spraying mud and water—his neck arching again, chest swelling as if to burst, as if an inner sun were on the point of exploding through it, the titanic effort clear in his bulging eyes and corded veins. His neck, cheeks, forehead glistened, streaked with sweat and mud and mist, his forelegs rose, neck and spine arching, leaping, falling, legs sloshing and plunging and staggering, and Wolfie was running along the plank, jumping onto the rush, calling out to him, and Dodo was screaming to Hero and clutching Wolfie and together they howled and hurrahed through the rafters of the evening.

Hero was on the rush.

He lifted his tail, shook his head, shook his withers, bent his knees, doubled his legs, and sank to the ground. He rolled and he rubbed his streaming flanks, rolling and rubbing and shaking, kicking and rolling, rolling and kicking, his four hoofs to the heavens.

Chapter Twenty-Eight

A long, hungry winter followed the summer.

Sergeant Box made his statement. The court-martial and the accusations against Pa were brought into the glare of public attention once again, chewed over once again, the children vulnerable to the insidious whispering of the village. The men talked of it in the pub; Mrs. Potter and her friends in the Village Stores gathered and gossiped. Wolfie had quietly given up his liking for Torpedoes and pear drops. Outwardly he minded less than Dodo about other people but he'd never gone back into the Village Stores. In London public and media interest in the case was ballooning. Box's statement, though in Pa's favor, did not commute the suspicion with which they were surrounded into warmth or kindness, but there would be an appeal, that much was certain. The court-martial had sharpened the tongues, ignited the talk of the villagers. Now the newspapers' interest in Box and his statement had brought everything to the fore once more.

* * *

One Sunday in February, at the breakfast table at Lily-combe, Father Lamb stared at *The Times* headline, shocked and silent. Hettie, in an attempt to be cheerful for the children, said, "Look, Wolfie, see how Hero clings to the ponies now. He so tall and gleaming, they so stout and furry."

Dodo managed a weak smile. Hettie had been so brave, saying only, "*Scout died where she loved to be, with you both and with Hero.*" She'd been so relieved to see the children home and safe and then so worried by her father's frailty, she'd not had time to grieve for Scout.

"Twenty-five thousand dead in one night," repeated Father Lamb out loud. He picked up Captain and turned him and turned him, tenderly, gazing at him from all sides.

"How the world has changed, Wolfie. Only yesterday it seems, we battled on horses, with lances . . . Now we can create six hundred acres of rubble, six hundred, in a single night . . . And our bombs may fall on statesmen, but they also fall on women and children, on horses and dogs. Why not daylight raids on military targets?"

There were tears on his cheeks. The children and Hettie were silent. The Allied air raids on Berlin, on Dresden and Hamburg, now once again on Berlin, had been thorough and devastating.

"Come, Father," said Hettie. "We must get you to church."

She helped him to his feet. Dodo went for his coat and hat and scarf.

Leaning on his daughter's arm, he said, "I'm finding the church a lonely place to be, Hettie. Twenty-five thousand dead. Can there be any justification for such a thing?"

"Shh, Father," said Hettie.

She looked at him anxiously. His congregation was dwindling. The village was uneasy with Father Lamb's anxiety, that anxiety being so at odds with the country's grim determination to get the whole thing over with, at any cost.

The sky was leaden. Inside Saint Simon's it was dark, almost as night. Hettie took her place at the organ, the children at her side, Wolfie to pump, Dodo to turn the pages. A solitary figure in black sat at the front in the pew she thought of as her own.

"There's Mrs. Sprig," hissed Wolfie.

"Pray for her, Wolfie," Hettie whispered. "Henry was killed."

Dodo and Wolfie bowed their heads.

Father Lamb lit a candle on the pulpit. He led the service, thin and frail and white, with a blanket draped over his cassock, the pale flame holding him as if in a pool of moonlight.

"Let us pray . . . ," he said, as the service drew to a close. When the shrunken congregation had bent to its knees, he continued, ". . . for the people of Dresden, for the people of Coventry, of Berlin, of London. For all whose lives have been taken by the bombings, for all human life must be valued."

There was a discomforted shuffling in the pews. Someone at the back rose and left, slamming the door. Father Lamb continued. The Causey family rose and left.

Father Lamb announced the final hymn, Wolfie's favorite. Hettie played the opening bars. Father Lamb sang:

"When a knight won his spurs in the stories of old . . ."

His voice was whispery and frail but no other voice rose with his.

"He was gentle and brave, he was gallant and bold,
With a shield on his arm and a lance in his hand,
For God and for valor, he rode through the land."

Dodo and Wolfie turned to the audience and sang, as fully as they could. Father Lamb's lovely baritone swelled with theirs and filled the church.

"And let me set free with the sword of my youth,
From the castle of darkness, the power of the truth."

He gave the blessing. They bent their heads. Wolfie saw Hettie's lips move and remembered to pray. Putting his hands together, he mouthed, "Dear God, Make Box well so Pa's appeal can be soon. Make Father Lamb better. Make people come to his church. Help me look after Hero." Then he ran out of things to pray for and mouthed, "Amen."

At the gate stood a dark clot of men. As Father Lamb stepped out into the porch, they booed and waved hastily improvised placards—

THE ENEMY STARTED IT.
WE WILL FINISH IT.

"God bless you," he said as he passed.

Later Hettie unplugged the Bakelite wireless set and hid the lead. Once again, she canceled the papers.

Chapter Twenty-Nine

Water froze in the taps, milk crystallized and froze in the larder. An elemental cold gripped the country, a cold to freeze the blood.

They woke on the last Sunday in February to a staring, unearthly radiance, white rime on stone and cobble, each blade of grass stiff, seed heads turned to silvery globes, branches bowed with crystalline ice flowers, electricity cables glassy and garlanded with blossom.

Father Lamb had died in the night.

"Dreadnought too," said Hettie, dark-eyed in the kitchen. "Dreadnought went with him."

Wolfie looked out of the window, down past Hettie's currant bushes to the graveyard. He smiled through his tears to think of Dreadnought and Father Lamb together at heaven's gate, of the rowan that would be there and of what God and Dreadnought would make of each other.

* * *

Father Lamb was buried next morning, with Dread-nought. They did not have far to go.

A myriad of diamond stars wreathed Father Lamb's rowan, each branch of it hung with berries that flashed like blood against so much whiteness.

Chapter Thirty

After the burial, snow, soft as wool, fell from a pearly sky. For thirty hours it fell, transforming the hills to ghostly waves, unreal and timeless.

There was no school, the children confined to the house, Hero to his box. Restlessly he barged at the door of it till he broke the latch and Wolfie tied it with twine.

Samuel came, on foot, through snow to his thighs, a pair of corn sacks tied over his boots.

"I'll bring the ponies in—they can't get to the grass," he called from the door. "Snow's too deep on the lane to get 'em here, but I'll get 'em into the shippon at Windwistle—that's big enough to hold 'em." He gestured to the sky. "There's more to come—sky's thick with it—any more 'n' it'll bury 'em."

'Do we have enough hay?' asked Hettie.

Samuel nodded. "Aye, and for the horse. For a week or two we've enough."

"I'll put Hero next to the ponies," said Wolfie,

watching Hero's fretful head swing from side to side over the door. "He doesn't like being on his own."

Samuel nodded. "Gi's a hand with the gates then," he said to Wolfie. "Ned's up there, rounding 'em up, but we could do with help on the gates."

Wolfie waited by the sheep pens at Windwistle, stamping and blowing on his fingers. Clods of snow thudded to the ground. The trees made strange creakings and groanings. Saplings snapped under their burden of snow with sudden, firework cracks. Wolfie was to keep one gate open, the gate on the other side closed. The ponies would be herded into the pen and the gate shut, from there they'd be ushered into the shippon.

He heard Ned's cussing and shouting, then a muffled pounding. The half-dozen ponies, their furry winter coats iced like Christmas ornaments, stampeded in a wild torrent at the gate, manes and tails flying. Wolfie leaped to one side, leaned flat against the stone bank, holding the gate open as the ponies streamed through, sending snow flying.

Ned and Samuel ran staggering behind them, keeping to the bits where the snow had been flattened, making guttural, animal noises, herding them like a sheepdog. The ponies pounded on down beneath the white arching trees.

"That's all on 'em. Shut it. Quick. Or they'll turn and stampede you."

Finding the bottom gate shut, the ponies came to an abrupt halt and whirled round. Finding themselves trapped between the two gates they became wild and frightened.

"Hurry, get that gate to the yard open," Ned called to Samuel. "Wolfie, get the shippon door open."

When they were all in, Samuel forced the frozen iron bar across its door, then tied baler twine around the top of it. "Can't rely on the latch," he said to Wolfie. "They can break their way out o' most places . . . put the horse in next door so he can see 'em. Give 'em all hay."

Samuel tested the door again.

"They're strong," he said, "strong enough to break through that."

"Aye," said Ned. "Keep the yard gate shut too. That way, if they get out o' the shippon, you'll keep 'em in the yard."

It was heavy work dragging hay over to the ponies and shovelling snow to keep the way clear, but the beech tunnel kept off the worst of the snow and made it easier to reach the shippon.

School remained closed. On the third day a stinging wind got up, whipping up the snow and rearranging it, building it up to the eaves of Lilycombe. Branches bent and broke, snapping like gunshot. Snowdrifts, eight-foot high, rose over the gates and filled every hollow. You could walk over the hedges not knowing they were there.

In bed, hearing the roof creak under its burden of snow, Wolfie thought of Hero in the shippon and was happy to think he was there with the ponies, warm and safe.

Chapter Thirty-One

The first drops of rain fell on the fourth night, an eerie drip, drip, drip, splattering and dimpling the snow. By morning it was swingeing and black.

There was a letter downstairs, from Pa, the first delivery since the snow had blocked the lanes. Something called a "Commission of Inquiry" was being opened by the Warwicks. Things were going Pa's way, the newspapers busy uncovering evidence, bit by bit, of what had happened at Wormhout.

Pa no longer added special notes for Wolfie. Dodo had written to him about Scout and probably because of that Pa no longer mentioned horses.

There was another letter, this one from Spud, on paper headed "26th (London) Antiaircraft Brigade." Wolfie padded around the kitchen, jam on his cheeks, a slice of bread in his hands, as Dodo read.

A Doodlebug—a flying bomb—had hit Number 25 Addison Avenue. It must have been a while ago because Dora was growing beans where it used to stand. Everything had gone, even the joists of it had been taken for firewood. Spud hadn't been able to save any-thing, but she'd found, in the front garden, a short-bread tin with Wolfie's cavalry inside. She said that the Doodlebugs looked like comets with trailing fire, that the roar and the rush of them could lift even her off her feet, and that she'd always known that the Captain could never have done what they'd said he'd done.

Wolfie, after nearly five years in North Devon, could barely remember Number 25 Addison Avenue.

The rain continued all morning, driving and re-lentless, washing away the white curves.

The door opened and Hettie stood there, white-faced, her tweed cape sodden.

"Hurry, help me. They're not there. Gone, all of them—Hero, the ponies . . ."

Wolfie held two fists to his mouth as though to stifle a scream. Dodo, deathly pale, walked like one already dead, towards the door.

The lane was running with water, the trees black and dripping. Pennywater howled down the little valley. The string to the shippon gate was gone, the bolt un-done. The yard, a foot or so underwater, was awash with mud, broken twigs, and sodden leaves. The two gates on the drang, the sodden wood of them, already corrupt, was breached in the middle. Numb with grief and fear, they gazed at the splintered wood, gazed questioning into each other's faces.

"The rain—there's no way of telling what happened . . . ," whispered Hettie.

They walked up beech tunnel and out onto the track that led up to the moor. The bushes there were trampled, impossible to tell now by what or by whom, but each sensed uneasily that there was or that there had been someone here. At the top, the gate to the moor was open, tied back in a secure and tidy knot.

"That was no pony," said Hettie, weighing the knot in her hand.

"Even Hero couldn't do that," said Dodo.

Hour after hour, they searched on foot, the hills and the valleys, hoarse with calling out across the black and sodden grass. To each other they said nothing, each haunted by the spectre of dark, crowded cattle trucks, the thought of what might have, must have, happened, too terrible to voice.

In the afternoon, Samuel joined them. Until it grew dark they searched. When they turned for home there was no Wolfie.

Samuel found him at dawn, shivering in the hollow of a gorse bush, and carried him back. He'd fallen from exhaustion, limp and brokenhearted.

Chapter Thirty-Two

"Never break faith with a horse, Wolfie."

Day after day Wolfie sat at the window, a lanky thirteen-year-old boy, holding the small lead figure he'd treasured since the day his father had gone to France to fight for his country a second time. The flesh-and-blood horse that was the embodiment of his own deepest dream was gone.

Hettie never mentioned the ponies again.

On the ninth of the next month, the wireless announced the bombing of Tokyo, a hundred thousand people killed. Hettie collected her coat from the hall and left the house, not coming back till nightfall.

By May, war in Europe was over, Hitler dead, but Pa remained in prison. Wolfie watched as Hettie dragged two huge old flags from the attic, last used for the Coronation, she thought. Dodo helped drape them from the first-floor windows.

The newspapers alleged, out of the blue, that an SS officer named Mohnke had committed a terrible massacre at Wormhout. Weeks later they said that a man named Otto Senf was responsible for ordering the massacre. Nothing could be proven because Senf could not be found. Once again Pa was in the papers, this time in connection with his statement. The papers whipped up a frenzy of anger and horror over the actions of the SS at Wormhout and a storm of indignation at the treatment meted out by the army to Pa.

In July, around a conference table in Potsdam, plans for the prompt and utter destruction of Japan were made. Hettie said she was glad her father could not hear such things.

That month they learned that Hettie was to lose her home, that in September a new rector would take the living. Numb at so much grief, all heaped together, Dodo thought only of Hettie when she asked, "Where will you go?"

Bravely Hettie told her that she'd go to her cousins in County Durham, that her uncle had always promised her a post at the village school there, that Dodo and Wolfie must come with her. She'd organized a post for Dodo as art tutor to her young cousins and Wolfie would attend her new school.

Wolfie, staring out at the empty box in the yard, did not look up.

Hettie and Dodo watched the haunted boy, their own eyes haunted by his grief. For Wolfie, as time went on, the loss had become harder to bear, the pain of it unassuageable. First, unbelieving, he'd searched all day, day after day, for the tall grey horse. As it grew certain that Hero, that the ponies, had gone, and gone forever, he was inconsolable. When once he'd begun to talk about Hero, about the ponies, about what might have happened to them all, he'd vomited with the horror of it. Now he never spoke of Hero, rarely spoke at all.

He'd broken faith with Hero. Hero had trusted Wolfie to look after him and Wolfie had failed.

"He must know you'll never let him down. Never, never break trust with a horse."

Wolfie told Dodo later that he'd never leave Lily-combe, that he couldn't go till he knew what had happened to Hero.

"We've no choice, Wolfie," Dodo told him.

Lilycombe was never the same to them again. When Hero went, when the ponies went, they'd taken the spirit of the place with them, torn Lilycombe up by its roots. Wolfie's heart had been ripped out of him, his dream stolen, washed downriver with the rain.

PART III

COUNTY DURHAM

Few men are willing to brave the disapproval of their fellows . . . Moral courage is a rarer commodity than bravery in battle.

Robert F. Kennedy, 1966

Chapter Thirty-Three

Wolfie waited at a crossing, as one coal wagon passed, then another. Two men stood outside the pub, cloth caps low over their heads, mufflers on their hands, faces dusted with fine black dust. Wolfie crossed and ran along the far side of the street to Wynyard.

He waited by the stately iron gates. Beyond the gates lay the stern gravel walk, the vast house, the gentle hills and mountains. Behind him stood a single row of houses in an importunate line, then the mining village, beyond that the tall chimneys and dark smoke. Below the mine lay the cliffs and harbor. Behind Wolfie, two women stood, waiting, on their door-steps, their faces drawn and tight, anxious for their men's payday homecoming. Rationing had taken an iron hold of the country, stronger than it had ever been during the war.

As Wolfie waited for Dodo, he fingered the letter in his pocket, finally taking it out and rereading it.

15 May 1946

Dearest Wolfgang,

So many birthdays have passed since I last saw you, so
many years I can never make up to you. The small boy I
once knew is now a young man. Fourteen years old,
Wolfie. You are now so used to jogging along without a
father that you'll have no need of me when I get out. I
don't mind my sentence on any account other than the
waste of the years I could have spent with you. I have to
guess what you have both become. At times I could tear
the prison bars apart with my bare hands to be with you.

I count the days to the end of my sentence when I
will see you both.

I try to imagine from your letters with what you fill
your days. Dodo is a better letter writer now than you
are. I miss your letters, Wolfgang, they were meat and
bread to me. There's nothing I can ever give you that
will make up for Hero, and certainly nothing I can send
you from this place. The only offering I have is to say
that my case will be appealed. I hope to be released
early and for the shadow over my name, over your name
too, to go. Vickers is of course released now, and both he
and Box have made statements on my behalf, we've

enough evidence for the appeal. The Warwicks, too, are collecting proof of the massacres. Unfortunately Mohnke is missing somewhere in the Balkans and Otto Senf is in hospital with tuberculosis, too ill to speak but since the SS make a vow of silence, a vow never to betray each other, I doubt he'd ever speak. Only when the bodies of my men are found will my statement finally be proved.

Dodo says that you help with the horses after school. I know you find some comfort there. The presence of a horse is soothing and healing.

I can't be at your side, but I am always, always, in my heart, with you.

Your loving
Pa

Chapter Thirty-Four

"What'll you do, Miss Revel, won't you come to tea with Father too?"

Dodo smiled and shook her head as she untied Cecily's art smock, adjusted Meriel's ribbons, and kissed the tops of their cotton-candy heads. "It's Wolfie's birthday," she answered, replacing their palettes on the trolley, wheeling their easels to the side of the gallery. "Your father said I might take him to the stables tomorrow. Will it make him sadder or will it make him happier, do you think?" She smiled. "Hurry. Your father doesn't like to be kept waiting."

The girls skipped down the gallery, ribboning like butterflies in and out of the marble statuary. Dodo untied her own apron and regarded, with a critical eye, the work of her charges. She sighed a slow sigh and turned to their subject, a bird of prey carved from marble. Guarded and wary, it gazed, stonily, back at her, all claw and beak, talons clenching its veined perch as though to pierce blood from the marble of it.

Dodo picked up a brush and corrected the claws,

her hand moving confidently over Meriel's more hesitant marks. Glimpsing the time, she put down her brush and ran to the door. She walked down the corridor, breaking into a tiptoe run where there was carpet, thinking, as she always did, that it took longer to get from one end of this house to the other than it did to cross the village.

At the gate she hugged Wolfie, feeling in his rigid arms the numbness in the center of him.

"We'll soon be home, Wolfie, we'll all be together."

"I know . . ."

Dodo took the letter Wolfie handed her. She read it and looked up and saw the longing in his haunted eyes. Her heart twisted with pain. How large Hero was still in Wolfie's heart, how very much he'd meant. Hettie said that he cried out in his sleep, that he screamed of trains, whiplashes, the press and crush of horseflesh in dark wagons. She said he'd asked once, when she'd woken him, if they'd been given water on their journey, if you gave water to a horse that would be butchered. Later she'd come to his room again to stop his screams and he'd asked how the thing had been done. With a gun? With a knife?

Hettie had answered Wolfie that the police statement had read: "Stolen. Loaded at Dulverton. Transported by train." That was all they'd ever know.

There was nothing Hettie or Dodo could give Wolfie, the darkness in him so heavy, so solid.

Dodo was taking his hand. Wolfie shook himself

with an effort to be cheerful for Dodo, who was being cheerful for him. Together, brother and sister walked the short distance to the modest terraced house that Wolfie and Hettie shared, the house that came with Hettie's post as assistant head to the village school.

Hettie was waiting in the kitchen. She hugged Wolfie. An iced cake stood on the table. Dodo put the kettle on the range. Captain, the small lead horse, stood in the window just behind the kettle. Dodo picked him up and held him, remembering Wolfie once, so small then, and so fierce. *"He will be brave and he will have a silver tip to his tail,"* he'd said as he'd lined up his cavalry on the table at Addison Avenue.

"And how is life at the Park? Does their drawing improve?" Hettie asked Dodo, who laughed by way of answer. Hettie joined them at the table and said, "Your pa's on a crusade—you know, for the miners—even now, even in prison . . . he seems to be drawn to difficult causes."

"Sometimes I think he writes more to you than he does to us," said Dodo, smiling.

"He's a brave man. The coal masters are powerful and stubborn. Your father's voice is a brave and lonely one. Moral courage is a rarer thing than physical courage."

"Hettie, if Pa—if Lord Seaton finds out what Pa is doing—"

"Your position at Wynyard will become untenable if he discovers who your father is."

Later, when the cake was eaten, the cards opened, Dodo saw that Hettie was grave and preoccupied.

"What is it?" she asked.

Hettie took a letter from her pocket and put it on the table for them to read.

Dear Miss Lamb,

Old man Jervis died last week. He died in jail, Miss Lamb. I thought you'd want to know. Having defaulted on the rent of the land at Windwistle and on Thorne, he's left his wife and children homeless. Young Ned's had a hard time. As the only provider for the family for a long time now, he was bullied by his father into some nasty goings-on. Caught at it by the police, he was forced, by the questions of a clever judge, to testify against his own father. I am sure I don't need to tell you, Miss, what some of those goings-on were, but it was clear that young Ned was bullied into them. The consequences for you have been terrible. When the good in him made him rebel against his father there was no more money

COMING IN FOR THE WEE ONES AND THE CONSEQUENCES FOR NED AND HIS YOUNG BROTHERS HAVE ALSO BEEN TERRIBLE.

IT'S NOT THE SAME AT LILYCOMBE WITH YOU GONE AND THE NEW RECTOR HAS NOT SO GOOD A VOICE AS YOUR FATHER.

YOURS EVER,

SAMUEL ROCK

Chapter Thirty-Five

The scent of oil and leather transported him, as if in a dream. Wolfie had a greasy cloth in his hand, a saddle on his lap. He could lose himself in the rubbing and polishing of a bridle, could lose himself in the brushing of a horse, but sometimes beneath his fingers there'd be the coat of another horse, the velvet of a young muzzle, the thistledown breath on his cheek. A wave of nausea would roll, gulping and choking from the pit of him.

"Learn him by heart, Wolfie, learn your horse by heart," Pa had said. And he had: He had the whole of Hero by heart, the touch of him, from nose to tail, the coat of him, the muscle and vein of him, all by heart, and if he closed his eyes, there in the tack room at Wynyard, he could run his fingers from the dappled neck to the silver tail of him.

Only Ryland and his yard could breathe some warmth and life into the boy. The old groom's father had worked in the mines, his son Jo worked there now. Wolfie would ask Ryland to talk about the miners' lives, to tell him what he knew so Wolfie felt close to Pa, close to the things that Pa cared for and fought for.

Ryland had been reluctant to have Wolfie's help when Dodo had brought him to the yard, but they'd grown accustomed to each other. Ryland found that Wolfie had a good hand for a horse, a soft hand. The boy had told him about his own horse and Ryland had softened, softened more when he'd seen the work was doing the boy good. To Dodo it seemed that Wolfie talked more to Ryland than to anyone else.

"Have you ever been down?"

Ryland was clipping Shannon in the yard. Holding her foreleg, he looked under her belly towards the boy and answered, "I never went down. Father was ostler in William Pit. Before I were old enough to go down, there was an explosion . . ." Ryland glanced across the park to the steam that rose from the distant winding shaft. "I never wanted Jo to go down, but there weren't no other work, nothing else but the pit."

"Does Jo like working there?"

"Well enough. But he never heard what we heard . . . After the explosion, then there were the flood . . . twenty-six men drowned . . . children, young as five . . . six hundred feet underground in a flood in the pitch dark."

"*Children?*" Wolfie asked.

"Aye, them're cheaper, women and children came cheaper than the men."

Wolfie hung up his bridle and collected another. Leaning against the door, watching Ryland at his work, he said, "My father writes speeches and papers for the miners. He's fighting to impose maximum working hours, maximum loads, and mechanical haulage."

Ryland straightened up and lifted his cap and looked at the boy. "Oh, aye? . . . And does the master know?" He gestured with his head to the house.

"I don't know. Dodo hopes he doesn't but even when Pa's in prison he's in the papers. He is contrary-minded. He doesn't think what other people think."

Ryland laughed. "Contrary-minded," he said, "is a fine thing to be."

"I don't want to be contrary-minded. I want to think what everyone else does, otherwise life is difficult."

"I see no evidence of you thinking what everyone else does," said Ryland. "Aye, an' your father's right, I'm thinking." Ryland moved to Shannon's off side and picked up a hind leg. "The men are paid piece work—paid, that is, for each tub o' coal. An' if you don't bring up enough o' them tubs, you can't feed the family. The country needs coal and wants it cheap, and the master wants profits, but the miner just wants a living wage. He's right, your father, the loads must be fixed at what a horse can carry. Fifty tons a day, them horses down there . . . fifty tons . . . or else a man can't feed his family. Fifty tons a day till their backs an' legs are broken an' they're shot where they fall. Or worse . . . Aye, hunger makes monsters of men an' a hungry man'll loose a tub of coal on a pony just to be given a faster one." He stroked Shannon's gleaming coat. "The master don't want change, he wants profit."

Shaking his head sadly, he went to the feed room to prepare the sugar beet for the horses.

Wolfie rose and wandered over to the window. He held the bridle in his hand, running his fingers across the metal bit of it, remembering the first time he'd put Hero to the bit, the young horse's indignation at the cold metal across his tongue.

When Dodo came down to the yard to find her brother, she saw him through the window of the tack room. He was tall now, she thought, older-looking than his years, tall and strong. She saw his finger move across the dusty pane. She saw the letters emerge, in mirror image.

OЯƎH

Dodo watched Wolfie sadly.

"Wolfie," she called to him, "I've got a picnic tea—we've ham and melon . . ."

"Melon?" Wolfie asked in wonder as he came to the door.

". . . And egg sandwiches, specially for you. I said every picnic had to have an egg in it."

"Every picnic has to have horses, and streams," said Wolfie.

Dodo tried again, holding out a pamphlet to him. "Look, Wolfie, there's going to be races—the pit ponies racing," she said. "It's their only week aboveground—the only chance to see them."

Ryland joined them, raising his cap to Dodo. He picked up the hamper at her feet, weighed it in his hand, disapproving.

"There's more in this than most here put on their table in a year."

Wolfie read the Pitman's Derby pamphlet, then turned to Dodo. "Do you remember the race, do you remember Comer's Gate?"

"I do, and I remember you flying about like a small bobbin!" She laughed.

"Nothing will ever be the same, Dodo."

Ryland took the paper from Wolfie's hand.

"Will you come, Ryland?" asked Dodo.

"No. I don't like to think on t'others, on them you won't see, as have the broken knees, the ones who can't breathe for the dust in their lungs, the stones in their guts."

Ryland put the paper back in Wolfie's hands and made for the tack room. At the door he paused and said, his back to them, "Them ponies pull tubs o' coal, seven tubs, seven tons, between rails half a yard wide, through pitch dark, their knees doubled a'most to the ground . . . No, you won' find me at them races."

"Hettie's asked me to go with her," said Dodo quietly.

"We'll stay here, you and I," said Ryland.

Wolfie nodded.

Ryland went about his work in the tack room.

"Come on, Wolfie, take the handle, help me," said Dodo, trying to recover the afternoon. She called good-bye to Ryland and they made their way out of the park.

"It would be quicker on a horse," said Wolfie, always resistant to walking.

At the park gates he looked doubtfully at the drear chimneys and brooding slag heaps, the Lilliputian houses that cowered in silent and bitter file.

"I miss Lilycombe," he said simply.

"I know, Wolfie, I know," said Dodo gently. "Nowhere will ever be as lovely."

"Do you think about it too?"

"All the time," she answered. "All the time."

Chapter Thirty-Six

1st June

Dear Wolfie,

The police have been in touch about the ponies of
Hettie's that were taken from Windwistle. As your
parent, they contacted me rather than you. I was of
course able to give them no information and they have, I
believe, now spoken to a man named Samuel. But I
discovered from them that the lease on the farmland at
Windwistle expired with the death of a Mr. Jervis.

That house, Windwistle, so close as I now know, to
Lilycombe, was your ma's childhood home.

I have bought the lease and made it over to you both.
Spud has made all the arrangements. It will always be
your home. This would have made your ma so happy.
One day, with Hettie's help, we'll rebuild the herd and

we'll find you a horse. In the meantime, no Jervis will ever set foot there again. We could all go there until Addison Avenue is restored and that may take some time since there is such a shortage of building materials in the country.

I heard something else, too, this week. Otto Senf, on his deathbed, broke his vow of silence. He admitted the massacre and the place of it. The bodies of my men have been found. It will be too late to make up the years I've missed with you, but it's now certain I'll be released early.

In all hope,
Pa

Wolfie put the letter on the table for Hettie to read.
"I couldn't ever go back," he said.

Chapter Thirty-Seven

A school holiday was given for the Derby. Wolfie went early to the stables at Wynyard, passing Dodo on her way to meet Hettie at the schoolhouse.

"Always put your money on a grey," Wolfie said to her.

He found Ryland washing down the immense dark horse the master had named Black Diamond. As Wolfie approached, Ryland leaned forward over the horse, his arms folded, head resting there, watching Wolfie, seeing the deadness in the boy's step and wondering. The boy had lost his mother, his father was jailed, the horse he'd had once had gone. Ryland saw the sadness in the boy.

"Nothing can't ever replace a horse you've really loved," he said as Wolfie came close.

Wolfie smiled and shook his head. He took the hose from Ryland, and the sponge.

"What happened to 'im?" Ryland asked.

"Stolen."

"Aye," Ryland said to himself, coiling the hose. "Aye,

an' they were takin' from all over in the war . . . an' after it."

Wolfie went to the tack room to fetch a towel. From outside he heard the determined tread of a boot on the cobbles, then a voice rising. When he came out, someone had Ryland by the collar, their two heads only a few inches apart, the hose water from the pipe spreading in a lake around Black Diamond's polished hoofs. Wolfie turned the tap off and coiled the hose.

"You tell 'im. You tell your boy. If he makes any more trouble he's out. If it weren't for you, an' my fondness for your father, your boy'd 'a lost his job a while back . . ."

Ryland submitted to the rant in silence. The man saw Wolfie. Reluctantly he relinquished his hold of Ryland's collar, turned, and made as if to leave.

"Who was that?" whispered Wolfie.

"Ostler from William Pit," answered Ryland.

"An' I'll tell you one more thing." The man had turned, was yanking Ryland round by the shoulder. "Once more and there'll be no work for 'im, if I find 'im at it again . . . It's a good pit, an' the men're happy an' I don't want no problems from your boy, makin' trouble where there ain't none an' stirring men up."

Ryland heard the man out, then said, "You won't lay a finger on Jo an' you know that well as I. You can't threaten me with what I know as you'll never do. You're too scared, Jervis, that I'll tell all as I know."

Wolfie sprang forward. "Jervis?"

The man kept his hold on Ryland and turned to Wolfie, considered him briefly then turned back as Ryland spoke.

"Them're expensive horses, if you 'as to buy 'em. But you don't buy 'em market price, do you? I seen you, Dick Jervis, aye, I know where you used to go, in the dead o' night . . ."

Eye to eye, Ryland watched Jervis. Discomforted, Jervis relaxed his hold on Ryland.

"To the siding, where the wagons stop. I seen you . . . I seen you unload 'em . . ."

Wolfie pushed between the two men, pulled Jervis to one side, and stood before him, eyes blazing. "Jervis?" he asked.

Jervis was silent.

"Aye," said Ryland, turning to Black Diamond. "Aye, 'e's named Jervis, Dick Jervis."

"What's Ned Jervis to you?" asked Wolfie.

Jervis looked slowly at Wolfie, narrowing his eyes. He turned to Ryland, then back to the boy, but made no answer. Wolfie leaped forward and grabbed him by the collar. Jervis, surprised to be manhandled by so young a boy, said after some consideration, "Old lame Jervis . . . Ned's father, that was . . . he was me brother."

"So Ned's . . . he's your nephew." Wolfie gripped Jervis tighter, shaking him.

Ryland, rubbing Black Diamond down, looked

over the horse's back, the twinkle of a smile in his stern eyes as he saw Wolfie thrust Jervis against the wall and pin him there.

"Ned Jervis sent you horses . . ."

Dick Jervis regarded Wolfie narrowly, his head tilted back against the stone. His eyes moved to Ryland, then back to Wolfie. "Aye," he said. "Ned sent 'em for the pit . . ." He paused.

Wolfie shook him; his head hit the wall and his face contorted. Wolfie waited.

"Me brother thought they went for meat, but Ned was soft an' thought more kindly to send 'em to the pits . . . They fetched the same money here as there, one way or t'other, so me brother knew no better."

His eyes still on the monster that was Jervis, Wolfie stepped back, stepped back in horror, stepped back in surging, racing hope.

"Double yer profit, don't you, Dick Jervis?" Ryland said casually, coolly. "Buy 'em off those wagons on yer own account an' sell 'em to the dealers at a profit. An' on the morrer, buy 'em same ponies back on behalf o' the master."

When Ryland turned to Wolfie, the boy had gone.

Chapter Thirty-Eight

Wolfie forced his way through the crowd, heart pounding, desperate, elbowing his way from one point to another, searching frantically for Hero, for Dodo, for the ponies. Where was he, where was she, where were they . . . ?

Ponies and horses were being led into a ring, bridled only, not saddled—bays, greys, roans, piebalds, skewbalds, furry mountain ponies . . . no tall and dappled grey. He ran round the ring, searching, pushing and shoving—more horses—more ponies, all sizes, all shapes—young boys mounting them . . .

At the bookies' stands, bets were being placed. To his right there was a small enclosure in which hill ponies were being shown by men in their gaudy best, and judged. Wolfie stopped. A small boy was fighting to control a feral and snorting thing—thick-maned, thick-tailed, mealy-mouthed—they were Hettie's—Hettie's ponies . . . *Where was Hero? Was he not here too?* Wolfie spun round, running, pushing, and stumbling. That was Hettie's brand, the "L" of Lilycombe, the "L" of

Lamb, the double "L" in the deep dark fur of the coat. He looked again—on one of them, two of them . . .

Wolfie called out blindly into the mass of men for Dodo. He called to Hero. Men turned and stared. Women stepped aside, still he was crying out like a madman, whirling and running, racing, searching for Hero.

In one place the crowd was surging up the sides of the horseshoe track, in another a brass band was booming—elsewhere, in a smaller ring, more hill ponies, redder, shorter ones, were being shown and judged. Somewhere else prizes were being announced, races called out, stakes shouted out.

Dodo, turning from a stand selling lemonade, saw her brother, ragged and breathless. She called to him, but he didn't hear. She ran to him and caught him by the hands and held him till he was calm enough to speak.

"They're here—they're here—Hettie's . . . Dodo, they're here—but not Hero—He's . . . he's not here . . . Where is he, Dodo, where is he?"

Later, back at Wynyard, Ryland was waiting for Wolfie.

"Jo—will he—I want him to take me down with him—I have to go down, Ryland—I have to . . ."

"Aye," said Ryland, smiling gently at him. "If 'e's down there, you 'ave ter."

Chapter Thirty-Nine

"Nod or grunt, no other sound, till we're through to the face and on our own. Nothing but your name."

Being with Jo was like being with Ryland, each of them the stamp of the other.

Wolfie reached the front of the queue. Through the window of the lamp cabin, he was passed a metal disc from a hook on the wall. John Anstey. The name of Jo's cousin, sick with the flu, was written down on a ledger. Wolfie was passed a heavy cylinder lamp across the metal counter. Copying the man in front, he hooked it on to his belt and joined a second queue, the awkward lamp banging against his knees, tools in one hand, and a lunch tin—a "bait" tin as Jo told him to call it—hooked to his belt. The line shuffled forward to the metal cage. They stepped in, a bell rang twice, and a steward called out, "Coming down."

From far below came an answer, distant, hollow, and chilling.

The cage was moving, barely perceptibly, down a duct, no more than six feet in diameter, the sides of it lined with wood. Wolfie looked up. The sun had not yet risen, but the darkness as they dropped was darker than the dark of the surface. The wood cladding gave way to sheet stone. The cage dropped faster now and Wolfie was dizzy with it. Down and down it dropped, the shaft black and bottomless it seemed.

Bits of coal and drops of water fell with surprising force on his face. The grey of the sky shrank to the size of his palm, the noise from above dying, the dark darkening. No one spoke. Wolfie clenched his teeth as the metal cage grated on the stone of the walls as it swung and bounced against them.

A dim light glowed below.

"Steady the basket," someone called.

There was a clanking of chain, then a sudden, violent thud as the cage hit the ground, flinging Wolfie against Jo.

"Six hundred feet down," whispered Jo.

Not a ray of light from the sky reached the bottom. Wolfie heard the metal bar of the cage being lifted. He made out the dark shape of a man, a figure holding a single light. The "overman," Jo said. Another man with a light and a map in his hands, a surveyor perhaps, approached the overman.

Both bent over the map and began to discuss the gradient of the new tunnel, the field above it.

Somewhere beyond the shaft bottom, in the tunnels, there were terrible crashes, clangings that reverberated and echoed, metal scraping metal, metal scraping stone.

"Wait till you get yer eyes in and can see summat," said Jo.

After a while they moved away, with the rest of the men, to collect a pick blade and tools from a pile.

They walked a quarter of a mile down a sloping roadway, known as a "drift," then turned into a passage, a declining tunnel cut into sheet rock, the roof arched and faced with bricks, the sides faced with bricks.

"Number Nine Branch Road," said Jo.

There were crossings at regular intervals. On either side of the tunnel stood workings, hollow spaces five yards or so wide, twenty deep, a supporting column in the center for the roof.

"Coal has a grain to it . . . like wood." Jo spoke less gruffly now they were away from the others, now Wolfie was safely down. He hadn't wanted to take Wolfie. He was holding his torch to the roof, whispering, almost with pride, almost with love. "Look, see the ferns? Preserved, like they were printed . . . three hundred million years old . . . each leaf perfect." He ran his fingers over the tiny leaves, the fronds patterned and overlaid like lace.

They branched into a tunnel that was so low and narrow that it felt like the inside of a black vein. It had high and low parts to it, wet and dry parts, their own torches shining like meteors in the thick blackness. The rumbling and clanking of trams in other districts shuddered through the walls.

"They say as this road's 'aunted. Someone died 'ere . . . a roof fall. Men say as if you see a lamp burnin', an arm holdin' it, an' no body at all, there's trouble . . . danger comin'.'"

Wolfie kept close to Jo. The alien, uncanny blackness of the air pressed on him like a weight.

"The whole of the town was above us in t' first passage . . . an' 'ere it's William Pit above our 'eads, and above William Pit's th'arbor. Just water and all them boats."

Wolfie preferred not to think about a whole pit and a whole harbor with its fleet of bobbing masts being above his head. "Is it far now?" he asked.

"Nay, pit's six miles east ter west, three miles t'other way . . . them's five hundred acres of George Pit under the sea."

Again Wolfie heard the curious pride in Jo's voice.

At 6:55 a.m. they arrived at the face they were to work.

"Eighty fathoms we are, eighty fathoms below the waves." Jo smiled and took off his jacket, waistcoat, and shirt. Wolfie shrank from the smell of the place, the dark of it, the heat and swelter of it. Jo saw and laughed. "Aye, headings are always the stalest bit of a pit. There's only the one way in and the one way out— the way we came." He took up his pick. "Come on, help at the back here, this is the end of the workings, this is where we start today."

"Where're the horses, Jo?"

Jo poked his lamp into the corners of the face.

"I'm testing fer gas," he said. "It can be touched off by a wee spark, e'en a pick'll strike a spark from a stone . . . Come on, jacket off. Get to. I'll take you to stables at snap time."

Later, when they paused to rest and wipe their faces and drink, Wolfie asked, "How many horses are there?"

"Forty-five on 'em, give or take."

"Are they far?"

"Aye, stables're always at the bottom. They're down one hundred fathoms." Jo set to at the face with his pick.

"Can't we go now?"

"At snap time the shift'll change—men coming in, men going out—when there's most men in the pit, we'll not be noticed."

Chapter Forty

Dodo was down early to the breakfast room. At her place lay an envelope, postmarked London, Waterloo.

Waterloo? London? Pa's hand on the envelope? Dodo tore at it and read, tripping and rushing in her haste over the words.

Wednesday

Dearest Dodo,

I'm released and on my way to London. I'll be with you both on Friday. I've to go to London first as I'm summonsed to the Prisoner-of-War Cage in Kensington Palace Gardens. I've only to identify the men of the SS that were there at Wormhout, then I'll come straight from Kensington to Seaton to find you both and bring you home.

I count the minutes.
In all haste & with all love,

Pa

Friday. Friday. Three days from now. Dodo was at the window, gazing out over the park, light-headed with joy, in a dream world of her own, when Lord Seaton and his manager entered, deep in conversation. Seaton nodded briefly to Dodo, introducing the visitor as Higson, his Consulting Engineer, then gestured for Higson to sit.

"How's the new seam? Is it good and thick?"

Higson remained standing, "Yes, sir. A good thick seam, a two-meter seam, sir. High quality household coal. But—"

The butler lifted the lid of a silver tureen.

Seaton helped himself. "Kedgeree?" he offered Higson, gesturing impatiently for the man to sit.

"The ventilation's poor, sir, and they found a fissure, a pocket of firedamp yesterday."

Seaton gestured again for Higson to sit. Higson sat but declined the kedgeree.

Seaton unfolded his napkin.

"I don't like it, sir, I want to pull the men out—deeper the seam goes, more likelihood of the firedamp—"

Coffee was served. Dodo took her place at the far end of the table.

"Do we keep going, sir, or can I tell the manager to pull the men off the job?"

Seaton unfolded his napkin.

"No," Seaton said. He sighed and speared a flake of haddock with his fork. "No, keep going just till the end of today. It'll make my life easier, at least for this afternoon, at the shareholders' meeting."

A glass of fresh orange juice was put in front of him.

"There's trouble ahead," he said, taking his fork to the kedgeree, as Dodo and Higson looked on in wonder and longing at the orange juice. "Trouble again in the House last week . . . I'd like to give those politicians some shareholders of their own, I'd like to."

Pa. Coming here. After so long. After five long years, they'd see the father they barely knew anymore.

The girls burst into the room.

"Morning, Papa," they chorused like little birds, then ran to Dodo. "Shall we sketch in the park today, Miss Revel?" they chirped.

Dodo smiled, bright and sunshiny because of Pa.

"It's warm, can we be outside—please, Miss Revel, *please* can we draw outside—in the park?"

The telephone rang in the hall. The door was opened for Seaton to step outside and take the call.

Dodo rose to help the girls at the sideboard. From the hall came Seaton's voice: "Keep the men on the job."

Chapter Forty-One

"Almost there," Jo said, as they ran down a side heading that lead from the haulage road to the pit bottom. Halfway along, where the heading levelled out, Jo gestured to a steel trapdoor. "Disused workings there . . . They gave up on those."

Wolfie glanced, for a bare second, at the trapdoor, then ran on impatiently.

"Too many roof falls, all faulty strata so they closed it up . . . ," Jo was saying, lingering by it. Wolfie stopped and turned, and saw Jo running his light along the edges of the door. Jo looked up at Wolfie. "My grampa died down there . . ."

At the end of the side heading was a cavern, lit with electric light, the walls whitewashed, the floor sawdust.

"See?" said Jo, as Wolfie gawped at the strangeness and the wonder and the horror of such a thing, a stable full of horses, with straw, with oats and electric light, all here, here beneath the surface of a sea.

"Better fed than the men," Jo was saying. "The master can get a man for free, don't need to buy 'im, but 'e 'as to buy an 'orse. An' that's a hefty thing today, the price of an 'orse."

Wolfie, not listening, broke away, shooting forward, running from stall to stall, horse to horse.

"Hero! Hero!" he was calling.

He didn't see Jo hold out a palm, turning his face towards the heading by which they'd come, didn't hear him say, "It's odd . . . ventilation's changed . . . air direction's changed."

Behind Jo, a lamplight was growing larger, picking its way through the gloom.

"Get on out," the figure said to Jo, moving on quickly. "Not along out-by, but in-by."

"Hero! Hero!" Wolfie was still calling, the name echoing down the stable, out into the long tunnel.

The figure with the lamp hurried on, the lamp dwindling away into the gloom.

"Hero! Hero!" Wolfie called again.

There was no answer.

A horse whinnied. Wolfie stopped. It whinnied again. Wolfie ran towards that voice but it was a tall dark bay horse who'd whinnied.

"Hero!" he called and he ran down the length of the stable like a man possessed, flinging himself from stall to stall, taking only the merest glance at each box. At the far end of the stables, Wolfie turned and hurled himself at the other side, caught the post of the box opposite and ran on down.

"No, no, no," he cried to himself as he reached the final box.

"Hero! Hero!" he cried softly into his hands.

He stood in silence, leaning against the wooden post, tears flooding down his cheeks, all hope gone.

There was a soft whinny. Wolfie covered his ears and buried his head in pain. Again a horse whinnied softly and there were soft hoof thuds on the sand floor. When Wolfie turned and looked up, a tall dark horse was being led down between the stalls towards him, his head high, almost to the ceiling, ears pricked and turning, the coat of him dark and black with dust, the mane shorn, forelock shorn . . .

In flesh and blood before him . . .

"*Hero! Hero! Hero . . .* ," he whispered.

The horse nickered softly. Slowly Wolfie moved towards him. Slowly he bent his face to the muzzle, smiling into the dusty velvet of it. He ran his hand up the head, along the shorn stubble of his mane.

"I'd know you . . . I'd know you . . . if you were covered in coal from head to toe, I'd know you."

He moved his hands over the bulk, the vein and muscle and tendon of the horse . . . all there, under his fingertips, as they'd always been.

Somewhere there were voices, shouts, screams echoing.

"Get out. Get out in-by!"

"Get on—get on—get out!"

He rubbed at the broad bone of the temple, brushing at it till the white of it was like a moon, the sweet dapple shining. Wolfie pulled and tore at the blinkers and hurled them down, then he smiled through his tears into the dark eyes.

"I'd know you . . . anywhere . . ."

They stood, nose to nose, lost to the world.

"Tie 'em up—help tie 'em all up—get the horses tied!"

Someone was running down the center of the stalls, pushing Wolfie to one side, saying, "Get th'orse in a stall—quick—tie 'im up."

Wolfie stood, detached from the commotion, fingering the dull coat, the muzzle and the dust-rimmed eyes, the pitiful stubble of his forelock, whispering to Hero, "I let you down, betrayed you . . . I didn't save you from this—"

"Get th'orse in the stall—tie 'im up I said!"

"I promise you, Hero," Wolfie whispered, "I promise you green fields and tall grass. I promise you rivers and mist and stars . . ."

Hero nuzzled him, then tossed his head impatiently. Tears slid from Wolfie's eyes. "Don't you know me? Hero, Hero—"

Someone cussed at Wolfie, pushing him to one side, yanking at Hero's collar, pulling him into a stall and tying him up.

"Wolfie!" Someone was calling from somewhere.

Wolfie followed Hero into the stall and stood by him, whispering, "I promise you bushes to scratch against and wind and . . ."

Hero tossed his head and pulled at his rope, eyes wild, swinging his head.

Jo was there suddenly, pulling Wolfie, yanking him, shaking him. "It's running the wrong way—air's reversed—we've got to get out." He dragged Wolfie out. "Give 'im hay—tie 'im up."

Jo ran into the next-door box, checking the rope, hobbling the animal. On the other side of the line, more men were doing the same, hurriedly working from stall to stall. Wolfie stood, stock-still, dumb and uncomprehending.

"TIE 'IM UP!" Jo shouted. Wolfie did nothing.

"You can't have 'em racing through the tunnels in pitch black. Tie him up. Quick." He grabbed Wolfie by the hand. "We'll get out down th'intake airway."

Wolfie stood his ground, shook his hand free.

At the far end, a flood of men poured down the passage that crossed the stables. Wolfie heard confused shouts, more men running, still more shouting.

"To the pit bottom! Get to the bottom!"

"By the haulage road of the second intake airway."

"Don't stop. Keep moving. Keep moving."

A door was jammed fast. Someone was forcing it with an iron bar.

"Get to the junction and out-by," someone shouted,

but Jo was arguing, urging, "No! Get along haulage road, into four-intake airway, to t'junction and out-by!"

Wolfie saw, as if in a dream, a train of lamps recede down the tunnel like a file of bobbins. Jo was running back to Wolfie. He grabbed Wolfie and shook him.

"For the love o' God, get out—there'll be an explosion . . ."

Terrified, Wolfie did nothing. He heard the squealing and shrieking of the animals, he saw them rearing and striking at the air, he saw their bared teeth.

"Get out—get out—I'll not stay with yer if you don't," Jo said.

Wolfie turned and calmly undid the knot that tethered Hero. Jo was pulling at him, Hero was squealing and tugging at his rope, sweating, trembling, shoulders and neck wet with lather. Wolfie had the rope in his hand, was turning Hero round.

Jo was screaming at him to get out, to tie the horse up, to run to the far end, to follow the men, that he was mad, that no one would stay with him.

Wolfie's world had slowed to a standstill, everyone grown swimming and dreamlike and otherworldly. He saw himself as if detached, from another place.

"No. No," he said slowly. "I will never leave him again."

Jo was suddenly at his side again, exasperated, yanking the rope from Wolfie's hand, fury and fear in his eyes as he tied a knot in Hero's rope and pushed Wolfie from the stall.

With immense and sudden force, Hero reared. The wooden bar of his stall cracked and splintered, whirling, dragging jagged wood in his rope, and he careered away, ears flat, the whites of his eyes round and wild.

Wolfie and Jo ran after him to the far end of the stables, where the rough roof hung in a low dark curve. Jo was shouting that they'd be killed—that they'd all be killed by a frightened horse in a dark tunnel—but Wolfie caught at his rope, and whispered to him, whispered and whispered, promising soft, sweet promises of grass and wind. Wolfie put an arm under Hero's neck, and looked into his eyes and made more promises he knew he could not keep.

"Come, come, Hero, come with me . . ."

Hero's eyes were large as night, the trust in them as stark, to Wolfie, as blood from a wound.

An almighty noise, like the sound of the sea, was gathering, a thundering like the roll of a wave. Then a blast of air, like an explosive force, broke and crashed through the chamber, rolling and echoing in waves after it, like a monster.

Wolfie was hit by the blast, picked up by it as if by a hurricane, and hurled down to the side of the tunnel. The drums of his ears were bursting, the air itself fluttering, his brain pounding with blood, his nose stinging, his limbs paralyzed.

He fell unconscious, a tremendous weight pinning him to the ground.

Chapter Forty-Two

"No, like this." Dodo took the charcoal. "Get the shape of her first." She sketched the head and neck, flank and quarters. "Afterwards you do the detail . . ." Lost in reverie, Dodo was drawing, not the horse that stood before her, but a different horse, dark-eyed, deep-necked, all white and grey and silver.

Meriel, fidgeting, held out her hand for the charcoal.

"Steady, Shannon, steady . . . still, now," said Ryland.

The seventeen-hand chestnut, all lacework vein and shivery skin, tossed her slender head. The girls took up their charcoal again. Ryland held out a handful of hay.

"Thank you, Ryland," said Dodo, checking the time. "And thank *you*, Shannon. Time to finish."

There was a distant muffled burst. Ryland started, turning to the distant chimneys. Shannon tensed, ears pinned pack, pulling at her lead rope.

"What's that?" asked Dodo, looking at Ryland.

Ryland's eyes were fixed in horror on the distant horizon. A steam horn sounded a loud, long signal, six short bursts, a long signal, and six more short bursts.

"What's that?" she asked again, taking up Cecily's charcoal.

Meriel didn't look up from her easel. "They sound that whenever there's an explosion," she said.

Still the steam horn sounded, over and over.

"What explosion? Where?"

"In the pit," said Meriel, scrubbing out a mark with her forefinger. "Don't worry, miss, it's only in the pit."

"Oh God . . . ," Ryland was saying, white-faced, turning to Dodo.

"Is he down there, Ryland?" she said, going to him, taking his arm. "Is your Jo down there?" She stretched out a hand to take Shannon's rope. "Go, go, you must go . . ."

"No, miss," he whispered. "Yes—that is . . . Jo is, an' your—your wee brother—"

"Wolfie?" breathed Dodo, aghast.

"Go there, miss," said Ryland. "Run an' I'll follow."

"Wolfie?" she whispered. "Wolfie?" She clutched at Ryland's collar. "Why . . . ?" she whispered, then she was screaming. "Where— Where is he?"

Ryland had turned, was running towards the yard, Shannon trotting airily at his side, Ryland calling over his shoulder and pointing, "Two miles, miss, it's two miles!"

Dodo picked up her skirts and ran.

Chapter Forty-Three

Someone was pulling him to his feet. His head was going to burst, his tongue was a plank, he couldn't swallow—there was no power in his lungs—he couldn't speak, couldn't breathe.

"Not hurt, s'all right, you're not hurt," a voice was saying.

The groaning and the roaring—was it the walls? Was it the very walls of this place? The floor of it beneath him, the whole workings—were they trembling and groaning? Was that Jo that was dragging him somewhere?

The beam of a light darted and jumped over the ceiling. When Wolfie's sight focused, he saw the quivering of a prop, a girder blown out and twisted, the gaping mouth of the roof, the stone fall behind.

"The haulage rope," Jo whispered. "It's off the overhead pulleys . . . Stay where you are."

Hero? Hero? Wolfie was groping through the dark.

"Hero! Hero!" he yelled.

Jo put a strong hand on his shoulder. "He's here,

Wolfie. Behind you, right here. He wasn't hit. Stay here a minute."

Wolfie tried to breathe, slowly in and slowly out, in and out, deep and slow.

"They'll be trapped like rats down there," Jo said. "The old workings'll be the only way to the mother gate—the old gate . . ." He grabbed Wolfie's hand, swung him round. "Drag the horse. He won't like it, but we've got to get in there."

He pulled Wolfie through the dark to what Wolfie thought was the entrance by which they'd come. Wolfie was tugging at Hero, feeling the resistance and the fear in him. He heard the screams of the tethered animals, hobbled and trapped and terrified. Jo had found a pick shaft, was telling Wolfie to take one from the rack by the door. He was bending and beginning to work at a closed door on the left side of the entranceway. Hero was whinnying and pawing the air.

"Get yer jacket off, tie it round 'is eyes—it's the shadows—'e'll be calmer maybe if 'e can't see the shadows."

"The others, Jo—the other horses—"

"Help me," was Jo's answer. "Got to get to the escape shaft of the old section—to the old road network." He put his pick down. "OK," he said. "Keep the horse back an' hold the light high."

He pried the door open.

A rush of stale air hit them with a blast, solid and

rancid as the breath of a tomb. They reeled in the force of it, recoiled, choking in the stench of it.

After a minute Jo uncovered his face and stepped gingerly into the opening.

"Hold the light up," he said. "Shine it onto the roof."

Wolfie ran his torch over the sagging ceiling, the twisted girders, a ways away a pile of fallen rock.

"It were bricked off, long ago . . . there was a fire— they bricked the face of it off to starve it an' it burned itself out. Come on," Jo urged.

Wolfie hesitated, eyeing the entrance, measuring its height.

Jo saw him and pulled him on. "Aye, high enough . . . horses used to work this road."

Wolfie stepped into the catacomb, retching almost with the stench. A sheen of moisture hung in front of his eyes. He pulled at Hero's rope, and the horse followed him in quietly, bending expertly beneath the entrance lintel.

"Always had faults in its geology. Even afore the fire, men always hated it more than any other district . . . Roof was always falling. Go on," he added. "Move on so as I can close the door." He took Wolfie's light and checked the battery. "I'm leaving mine here on t'other side, so as they'll see . . . anyone'll see, if they come, to follow this way."

He dragged the door closed behind them.

Chapter Forty-Four

Other figures, white-faced and haggard, converged on the road to the top of the hill. Hundreds more were running up the brow towards the pit yard and winding gear.

Dodo reached the stark black tower where the crowd was concentrating, a dark clot already pressed to the pit-head gate. Below, to the seaward side, more figures were rushing up the streets that climbed from the harbor, a whole community running.

"Two shifts down there," someone at her side was saying, "those going in-by and those going out-by."

"One hundred and fifty of them down there," another answered.

"Shaft's burned out."

Dodo saw what they called the shaft, the smoke pouring from it, nearby a cabin, and three men in suits talking. The crowd was pressing behind her, more than five hundred perhaps. She forced her way through to the cabin, straining to hear what the men in suits were saying.

"Shaft Two?"

"Destroyed."

"Three?"

"Wasn't working before and won't be working now. No way for 'em to get to it anyway."

"They're trapped then."

"Aye . . . We 'ave ter wait for a new cage."

"Get volunteers for a rescue party."

Wolfie, Dodo was thinking. Wolfie . . . Oh, Wolfie.

"A'most three miles, the fire's near three miles from the down-take shaft. If Shaft Two isn't working, they're trapped—there's no way out . . ."

Dodo heard someone speak the words as if through a pounding sea, as if the sea were in her head, churning and crashing.

"They'll be trapped . . . it'll be a wall of fire down there and they're behind it . . . No way out."

Wolfie trapped behind a wall of fire. Trapped in an exploding mine two miles from land, a hundred fathoms below the surface of the sea . . .

When Dodo came to, she had a blanket over her shoulders. Someone put a cup of tea in her hands.

"My brother—" began Dodo.

"My son," said the woman with the cup of tea.

The sun was setting across the harbor. The woman told Dodo that a replacement cage had arrived.

The sky darkened. Soft drizzle began to fall. Still more people were joining the crowd on the brow. The foreman called for a party of volunteers, for eight men. Ryland was the first to step forward.

Dodo went to his side. "Take me down with you," she begged.

"No, miss."

"If you don't return within an hour, a second rescue party will be sent down," the foreman said as the men stepped into the cage.

Chapter Forty-Five

The cone of light showed an opening in the side of the tunnel, now bricked up. Behind it lay an old coal face.

"There's no other way," said Jo. "From there it's two miles to the old shaft."

Wolfie leaned in to Hero's neck, feeling the horse's uncertainty. He held his head to Hero's muzzle and breathed deeply, slowly, in with Hero, out with Hero.

"Can we get through?" he asked when the horse was calm.

"Aye, an' it's the only way we'll get out . . ."

Jo took up his metal bar and crouched. Wolfie held up his light for Jo to see. Jo forced the bar into the crumbling mortar and pried out a slightly loose brick. He ran his hand around the gap, then prodded the space behind with his bar, tapped the brick behind.

"Two," he said. "Two bricks deep."

Whispering to Hero to stand, Wolfie crouched. One by one, brick by brick, they unpicked the face of it, leaving the second layer.

"Go careful, slow and careful . . . Might be firedamp on t'other side. An' if there's damp . . ."

Jo paused and wiped his brow.

"Then what?" asked Wolfie.

Jo shook his head. "We brick it up quick."

Wolfie poured some water from his bottle into the palm of his hand for Hero. Hero snuffled and snorted. Water ran over the edges of Wolfie's palm. He remembered the dark stable where a small foal had slurped milk and honey from the palm of his hand.

"How much water do you have?" Jo was asking.

"Half," said Wolfie. "Half my bottle."

In the light of his lamp Wolfie saw Jo's smile, a sad, charmed, exasperated smile.

"Don't go givin' it all to the horse."

"How high is the tunnel, Jo?"

"High enough. It were one o' the main road workings—where the big horses worked. The condition of it's maybe going to be more o' a problem."

They set to again with their picks.

"They knew," Jo said when they paused again to drink and rest. "Management always knew it were prone to spontaneous combustion. Seven hundred men killed, that day, the day my grampa died . . . it were like today, two shifts in t' pit . . ."

"What will happen to us, Jo?"

Jo stretched a cut and bleeding hand across his face, rested his head against the wall. "I'll bore a hole and test for damp. If the air's all right . . ."

Wolfie was outside, seeing himself as if from far away. A boy in a mine, with a horse. A wall of fire to their backs. The only way out down a road on which seven hundred men had once died, a road that was liable to explode suddenly and violently and unpredictably.

He rested his head against Hero's neck and whispered, "You're two miles out to sea, a hundred fathoms below the waves, and you must break through a brick wall into a tunnel. You don't know if there's firedamp in there but it's your only way out . . ."

It felt better to say it.

" 'E trusts you, an' all." Jo smiled, watching. " 'E— look at him, so calm 'e is—'e trusts you to get him home safe . . . an' 'e's looking into the belly of you, so get that pick—hold your lamp up for's—best keep going, quick and steady, no panicking or rushing at it."

Later, while they waited to catch their breath, in the stillness they heard a distant roar.

"The others . . . everyone else?" asked Wolfie.

Jo shook his head slowly.

Chapter Forty-Six

The sky over the sea deepened. Grim lines were carved on stern, lamplit faces, all eyes following the dense smoke that poured from the shaft.

As the cage was winched to the surface the crowd started forward. Immediately it was pushed back to make way for the stretchers to be carried out.

Two bodies.

The rest of the rescuers stepped out, black-faced, coughing and choking. Dodo saw Ryland among them. Wiping his face with the back of his hand, he spoke to the foreman, shaking his head slowly.

"Ten at the foot of t' shaft . . . too late—bodies . . . cage mangled . . . can't get through. Tubs off the rails— roof props blown out—"

The foreman shouted over him. "More volunteers needed to bring 'em up."

People surged forward—men, women, and children.

"No, Don't go— No!" Ryland was shouting, waving at them, pushing between the crowd and the shaft.

"There's a change in the air current. I tell you, don't go down."

The younger men looked at him and shook their heads. The foreman picked fifteen men. They grabbed at helmets, loaded timber and rescue gear.

"I tell you, don't go down!" Ryland was still shouting at the crowd.

The men in the cage looked at him silently as it began to drop. Ryland rushed to the foreman, grabbing him by the shoulders. "Any survivors will be at the bottom—you can't get to 'em now—there's a change in the air current. Get everyone out, get 'em out, I tell you, man, get the cage up!"

Dodo was forcing her way forward to Ryland, grabbing at him. "What does it mean? What's a 'change in the air current' mean? What's going to happen?"

Ryland watched the cage drop and said quietly, "Each one of 'em's a brother or a father or a son down there . . . they'll not listen." He turned back to the foreman.

Dodo pleaded with him, tugging at him, begging him to tell her what would happen, but Ryland turned to the foreman.

"I tell you, man, get 'em out. Get 'em to bring up bodies at the foot o' t'shaft and go no further."

The Salvation Army was setting up trestles, handing out tea, coffee, and blankets. Dodo, shivering with fear, found her hands were trembling so much that she couldn't raise the mug to her lips.

"Dodo."

It was Hettie. Dodo fell into her arms.

"Wolfie?" Hettie asked.

There was a violent boom. The earth shook under their feet. Flames shot a thousand feet into the sky. Fumes bellied out. The crowd fell back in horror and fear.

"What's happened? Hettie—what's happening?"

Ryland's hands covered his face.

After a while he said, his face ashen, "There's no hope, no hope for any of 'em, miss . . ."

Chapter Forty-Seven

Wooden beams and archways, snapped or twisted out of shape, appeared and disappeared in the swinging arc of Wolfie's lamp.

"A mile thereabouts to go. Shade the light—the further the horse can see, faster he'll go, an' if he puts a hoof on the rails he'll slip and fall and break his knees. Make 'im go careful. Swing the light up to the ceiling now for me."

"Collars are all right, mostly they're high—'e won't have to bend . . . an' men prefer the old beams to the new iron ones. Wood creaks, creaks an' groans like an ol' tree afore it collapses, them new iron ones just snap out, sudden, like bullets."

Wolfie kept a hand on Hero's neck, the warmth and strength of it a comfort.

"Half a mile, near enough, to the old shaft," Jo said.

There was no firedamp in the tunnel, Jo had said, but the thickness of the dark was sinister and uncanny.

They moved on through it, on and on. Hero was

beginning to tire perhaps, or finding the ground difficult. Beneath the palm of Wolfie's hand, the skin of his neck was growing hot and sweaty, his occasional refusals to budge the more frequent. Wolfie whispered to him, but the skin under his hand was as tremulous as the surface of a stream.

The horse's fear transmitted itself to Wolfie and surged like a hot current through his own veins. Suddenly Hero yanked up his head and pulled back, dragging Wolfie with him. He whinnied wildly. The shriek echoed and spiralled in the black cavern. He spun round, snatching the rope from Wolfie's hand, metal hoofs clattering on metal rails, the bulk of him a whirling mass, sudden and terrifying. Wolfie glimpsed the rump of him, then the flanks, catching Hero's neck now in the arc of his lamp, a feral, flaring colossus, unpredictable and terrifying in the confined darkness of the tunnel.

Wolfie's calls to Hero, the ringing of metal hoof on metal, and the horse's squealing whinnies all whirled and eddied in the black.

"It's all right, 's'all right, Hero."

The arc of his light found the horse and Wolfie saw the whites of Hero's eyes, his head high, almost to the ceiling, electrified, febrile, and overwrought. One foreleg pawed and struck the air.

"Shh, it's all right, Hero, s'all right," he said again, but his own voice wobbled and shook.

"Shh, hold 'im still," said Jo. "Quiet . . . an' listen."

Jo took Wolfie's lamp and walked on carefully, the beam of it swinging, disembodied and ghostlike, in the wall of dark.

"Stay still—don't move."

They waited, Wolfie and Hero distant from Jo by twenty or so feet.

"Stay still," Jo said again, creeping back towards Wolfie. "Stay where you are."

They waited a while, together in silence, on either side of Hero.

Suddenly there were running steps, voices, two lights coming from behind them.

"Thank God," Jo said. "Thank God . . . some of 'em've come this way."

Five figures appeared, one wounded in the legs, supported on either side, all of them weak and coughing, their eyes large and white in their grimy faces.

They exchanged a short, grim greeting with Jo, nodded to Wolfie and Hero.

There was a distant boom, a muffled, faraway roar.

"Did you hear that—did you hear?" Wolfie asked. "What's happened? What's happening?"

"Another explosion—at the main shaft head perhaps . . ."

Jo shook his head slowly from side to side. The men were silent, heads bowed for many minutes. When one of the older men looked up, his black cheeks were streaked with tears.

After a while, Jo rubbed his eyes and looked up. "That's what were bothering 'im," he said. "Horse knew it were comin'. Wait for a bit, then we'll go on."

An hour or so passed, then one of the older men nodded to Jo and they all went on in silence. Wolfie's hands trembled on Hero's neck. His legs were shaking, tripping and stumbling as he followed on behind Jo and the men. Hero was light on his hoofs, live and wary.

"Come on, steady the horse, calm 'im, we 'ave to keep going," Jo called.

"Come on, Hero, come on," Wolfie whispered, watching their lights, scared of being left behind, of the men going on ahead into the darkness and leaving them alone. He pulled again at Hero, but the horse was hesitating, pulling back on the rope. Wolfie breathed deep and slow to stop the pounding of his heart. The men's lamps were growing smaller. Wolfie tugged again.

Hero pawed and snorted and pranced, striking the air with a foreleg. Wolfie's arm quivered as he tried to pull him on.

"Come on, Hero, it's OK. The explosion was by the main shaft . . . a long way away."

Again the horse demurred.

Wolfie waited. His body quaked from top to toe. He heard a faint and sinister creaking, like the creaking of a ship. He held his lamp up to the ceiling. Nothing. He took a step back, still holding the lamp to the ceiling, then another step, and another, the horse moving quietly back with him. He saw a long and vicious crack.

"Get back!" he yelled. "Get back, get back!"

Hero whinnied, a piercing scream of terror that stretched and echoed like a wild thing down the tunnel. His hoofs struck the rail, again and again, pawing and jabbing.

"Get back!" Wolfie was shouting. "Get back, get back!"

There were running footsteps, men shouting and calling to one another, Jo's voice screaming, "Get back! Get back far as you can—Run!"

Hero was huge and whirling, monstrous and sudden. Wolfie tried to steady his lamp, still calling out to the men, but Hero was plunging up and down now, swinging his head from side to side, a gleaming colossus, all running sweat, eyes bulging and glinting. Suddenly Wolfie was thrown backwards, hit with force in his side by the great bulk and bone of Hero's head, and flung to the ground.

Men were shouting and screaming and running past him. Wolfie lay, coiled in pain against the wall of the tunnel.

There was an immense boom and Wolfie wound himself tighter, buried his head in his arms, blocking out the roaring, the screaming . . .

There was another boom, more screaming, then the crash and thunder of falling stone.

Choking on the rush of vile air, his mouth gritty, eyes stinging, the air thick with dust, Wolfie was numb with terror. Ahead, somewhere in the dark, stone was sliding. He tried to stand but his legs had turned to water. Shaking violently, he groped for the fallen lamp, spitting dust and grit. Clutching it, raising it, he saw a mound of hard grey rock and debris.

Behind him there were voices, then ahead a cry—the sound of a man groaning in pain. Wolfie leaped forward, his hand shaking with such violence that the beam from the lamp jumped and swung across the darkness. There was another rumble, a further slide of stone far ahead, the dust of it clogging his eyes, his mouth, choking his throat. He spat out more grit as he turned: There in the violent shaking of his beam was the horse, large and spectral; and behind him were figures staggering and stumbling, clasping each other. Swinging his lamp the other way, Wolfie called to Jo.

Wolfie called again.

There was no answer. Wolfie stepped forward, the beam of his light useless in the thick dust. He waited, glancing towards Hero, sensing the horse's wariness, seeing the watchful eyes, the tense ears, the blindfold gone.

"Jo!" Wolfie called, his mouth dry. "Jo!"

Hero stepped forward, nuzzled his hand, his shoulder, pushing him. Wolfie paused, then rose, steadying himself with a hand on Hero's neck. He held out the lamp. In its beam, dust swirled.

Holding a clump of the shorn mane, Wolfie moved cautiously forward. Hero moved with him, careful as a cat over the fallen stone, which littered the rails, his steps sure and true in the dark. Wolfie went on, stumbling, conscious of the horse's alert intelligence, wary and sharp as a wild thing, conscious of his own soupy brain. Behind them rang footsteps on the metal rail, making their own way on.

How high was the fall? Had it blocked the roadway? Jo? Wolfie stumbled into a rock, hitting the bone of his knee, the sudden agony of it doubling him up. Hero was snorting, stepping away, treading gingerly across the sharp stones to the right, live and wary. Wolfie lifted his lamp. Had the fall been only on the left side? He saw the curve of the tunnel. To the right, the wooden prop, creaking a little, was bent but holding. He swung the beam up across the curve of the roof. The center was holding, to the left a gaping hole, a pile of stone and debris beneath the split and jagged props.

"Jo! Jo!"

His voice was a desperate scream. He swung the lamp to and fro over the fallen rock.

"Here . . . I'm here . . ."

Wolfie started forward, stumbling over the rough stone, several hundredweight of it. The lamp swung back and forth. He was scrambling round the slagheap, falling, sliding, scrabbling at it with his bare hands.

"Where, where . . . ?"

He stopped, horrified.

"My chest . . ."

Wolfie knelt, wiping the debris from Jo's face with his own filthy hands, tears streaming down his own cheeks. Jo was clear of the main landfall, lying sideways across the tunnel, a rock pinning down his chest and one arm.

Wolfie moved tentative hands towards the sinister black mass, broad and flat-bottomed. How had Jo not been crushed to death? How could he move it? Was it more dangerous to move it than not? Wolfie lifted Jo's free arm and placed it above his head. He called out into the blackness—"Help, help!"

Someone was moving through the dark to reach them.

Wolfie placed his own hands on either side of the stone, weighing the size of it. He called for help again.

A voice called back to Wolfie to "Wait!"—that two of the men had lost consciousness from the after damp they'd tried to escape earlier, that they had to be carried, that Wolfie should go ahead and get help.

Wolfie waited. For a long while he cradled Jo's head to his chest, holding his limp, cold hand in his, his own head bowed. When Wolfie looked up, the older of the men was at his side.

"Go on, laddie. Hurry. I canna leave my boy. For the love of God, go on, get help for's."

Chapter Forty-Eight

Twenty hours had passed since the last explosion. The engine house was a tangle of bricks and twisted head-gear. New winding apparatus and a new cage had been driven up.

A pair of bodies came up in the cage, the arm of one wound around the other. Tear stains streaked the coal dust of their cheeks. Other bodies, already up, lay in carts, scorched, all clothing burned away, hands lifted to their faces, now forever, some had almost no aspect of humanity left. Later, all of them were covered in straw and carried away, by horse and cart, followed on foot by silent mourners.

"Wolfie, Wolfie," Dodo whispered to herself, over and over, hallucinating with exhaustion and cold.

A team went down to examine the shaft and pit.

Two hours later they returned to the surface. The main road had been impassable, the West Return impassable, the whole area quivering and quaking. No one in-by could've survived, they said. The Area General Manager arrived and issued an instruction to make a road through the fall, to work with the utmost speed and explore the airway from the Seven Quarter Second South District. This passage might connect with the East District return drift where it crossed the Seven Quarter Seam.

Two rescue workers were brought up on stretchers, their companions reporting that props and doors had been blown out, but that this passage could be travelled.

Later still, another report came that the East District return drift had been reached, but that they could go no farther without rescue apparatus, as the air crossing was damaged.

Dodo listened, numb and uncomprehending, one of the hundreds still waiting there.

The manager called for twenty volunteers. A hundred or more men stepped forward. Those who stepped forward were asked to dig graves.

Hettie brought Dodo a blanket, a fresh cup of tea.

Ryland knelt, and took Dodo's hands.

"They were together—your brother an' my Jo—they were . . . they—they 'aven't . . . they were working on a different face. The fire crossed trunk road and that road crosses all t'other in-by faces that are being worked an' all the roadways . . . all on 'em, 'cept the old closed road—that one's sealed off." He looked up at Dodo. "My father died down there . . .'e used to work that road—"

Ryland broke off, seeing men arrive at the surface, pouring out, all shouting.

"Smoke coming out o' brickwork . . . Doors to t'airlock blown out . . . Separation doors burning . . . Too hot to breathe . . . The dust chokes you."

Two men were carried out of the cage unconscious. When they came to, they vomited.

Chapter Forty-Nine

In pitch dark, Hero and Wolfie picked their way between the metal tracks. Most of the lamps had been lost in the rubble. Wolfie had left his, the only lamp remaining, to the two men who stayed with the wounded. Old Walter Hobbs, the oldest of them all, was unconscious, all of them coughing and choking on the gas that was in their lungs, burns on their hands and clothing.

Trusting Hero to lead him, Wolfie followed at his side, terror at every step, his throat parched, barely daring to breathe for fear of gas, for fear the air itself was poisoned, the roof about to fall.

How far it was, Wolfie barely knew. "A *cord*," they'd said, there'd be a cord. But the shaft had not been used in so long, and how could they know if the cord would still be there?

"Go on," they'd told him. "Go on and get help. Pull the cord at the bottom of the shaft."

Wolfie felt the gentle ticking of Hero's pulse, the solid warmth of him, and he could hear the dripping of the walls. He had no other senses—he'd only his fingers and his ears, only touch and hearing.

"*Courage is when you have no choice*," Pa had once said to Wolfie. He'd said that he wasn't brave, just that there was no other option. At Moreuil Wood there'd been nowhere else to go but into the enemy fire. Wolfie had never thought about those words of Pa's until now.

We have no choice, thought Wolfie now. This is our only hope. Eighty fathoms or more beneath the surface, in a tunnel prone to collapse, we must find our way in the dark to a shaft that may or may not be working.

"*Courage is nothing more, Wolfie, than when you can't not do something, when you've no choice.*"

That was what Pa had said, when Wolfie had been sitting on his knees, by the fire, the medal in his hand.

Wolfie fumbled onward through the dark.

Chapter Fifty

By late afternoon the following day, all hope was abandoned. Men were sent down once again, but only to recover bodies. Hour after hour, more deaths were known for certain, more women led into outbuildings to identify them.

The vigil had lasted three days and ended for all in heartbreak. The silent crowd on the pit banks and in the colliery yard watched and waited.

Processions wound through the town, a Davy lamp on each head, the haunting sound of "Gresford," the miners' hymn, drifting upward.

Chapter Fifty-One

Wolfie lay curled like a small child, tight against the curved wall of the old shaft head, face to the dirt. Hunger and fear clawed at him like nails. Fearing to breathe, fearing to give in again to sleep, Wolfie clutched his arms around his chest, fearing the clotted blackness, the ghosts that must haunt such a place, fearing the men to whom he'd given false hope, the men who could walk no farther, whom he'd left, promising help.

There'd been no cord.

When he woke again he heard the eerie dripping of the walls and a strange new rasping sound. His clothes were wet, his tongue clumsy and dry, his limbs shaking. He stretched a hand through into the darkness. His fingers found something . . . Hero, Hero's leg. Wolfie ran his hands up, struggled to his feet and stood, clutching at him, trembling over the warmth of him, clinging to the comfort of a living, breathing being.

Standing, leaning his own head against Hero's neck, he listened to his breathing, to the jaws, grinding and chomping.

Wolfie started, then ran his hand down the head over the loose muzzle. He started again, searching with his fingers from the muzzle and found only the rough surface of the wood . . . the gnawing . . . Hero was gnawing the wooden posts. Wolfie ran his hand over the grain of it, stretched out, backwards to the wall, ran both palms over the stone of it, felt its dripping wetness.

He heard a tongue rasp against stone and he whirled round. The horse's head lowered and snuffled the boy's hand, placid and curious.

"Oh God . . . Oh God." Wolfie's tongue was dry and thick. "How long've we been here?" he wondered. He cried softly into Hero's neck. "I promised—I promised green grass and mist and stars and trees to rub against and stars . . ."

Hero lifted his head, and he laid it over the boy's shoulder and let it rest there.

"There's nothing on earth like the moment a horse rests his head on your shoulder."

Fresh tears streamed down Wolfie's cheeks. The deepness of the gesture, the trust in it, felt, to Wolfie, like the twisting of a blade in an open wound . . .

He shook himself free and ran a trembling, feverish hand over the rough wall, following the curve of it, reaching blindly out in the thick blackness, both arms outstretched, searching, tripping, and stumbling like a madman through the dark.

Chapter Fifty-Two

The colliery yard was still thick with silent figures. All listened, heads bowed, as the Secretary of the Mine read a list of the missing and the lost: name after name, three men to one family, four to another. Not a man, not a street in the town was untouched, in every house a son or brother, a father or an uncle lost.

A long silence followed.

In that silence a bell rang out.

Again and again it rang, frantic and feverish. Sudden, spurting hope electrified the faces of the crowd. It started forward. Ahead of them all, Ryland was running up the hill, shouting, "The old shaft—Number One shaft!"

Men ran after him, the foreman dropping his paper, running, too, shouting for a cage, for machinery, for temporary headgear. Dodo was running, racing with the crowd, joining the flood that poured from the main shaft to the next brow, trying to find Ryland.

* * *

On the lip of the old shaft, men were calling down, their faces wild with hope, torches flashing into the darkness below.

"Send me down!" Dodo cried. "I must go down."

Someone was pulling her back and saying, "There's no way to get down."

She broke free. "Send me *down!*" she screamed.

The foreman called for quiet, for silence, for everyone to keep calm. They waited, breath held, listening, but their silence was met only by the silence of the grave.

"Send down a bottle—any bottle . . . brandy . . ."

Machinery was being hauled up the banks. A hundred desperate hands were rigging up a makeshift headgear. A brandy bottle was passed from hand to hand.

Ryland tied the bottle to a rope and lowered it.

On and on, he fed the rope, five hundred foot or so, into the greedy, unfathomable dark. Then he waited.

"Pull it, man, pull it!" people begged him after a while.

Ryland waited a little, then began to pull. Five slow minutes passed. Men's, women's, children's faces were lit with hope. Still Ryland was hauling up the rope. As the end of it neared the surface, one by one they stepped back, shaking their heads.

Ryland fell to his knees, bowed his head, and pulled, hand over hand, just for the sake of it, knowing there was nothing there.

"There's nothing—nothing . . . ," he croaked.

"Keep going, man, keep pulling!" the crowd shouted.

Ryland pulled, mechanically, like a dead man, the last twenty feet of rope to the surface.

Dodo saw, illuminated by a hundred torches, a plume of silver tail hair, knotted in the end of the rope, like a sheaf of moonlit wheat. She leaped forward, grasping the rope, clasping it, holding it to the light, raising it to her mouth, to her cheeks.

"Wolfie!" she screamed. "Wolfie!"

Ryland was at Dodo's side. She looked up at him, held up the silver plume, and whispered brokenly, "The horse . . . It's down there . . . Wolfie's there . . ."

The headgear was in place, the rigging in place, a hundred desperate men pleading to be sent down.

Later it began to rain. The cage had been lowered over two hours ago and still there was silence from below.

For a long time, the wheels turned. The sky greyed.

A motorcar drew up below. The crowd turned to watch as someone stepped out and began to climb towards the old shaft. The crowd turned as one and stepped aside, silence falling as he drew close, a path opening to allow Lord Seaton through to the shaft head, the murmuring and muttering in his wake like a rising sea, the swelling hostility of it palpable. The crowd tightened and closed behind him and he was caught in its web. Grief gave way to a surge of wholesale anger.

Dodo, uncaring, turned back to the shaft head.

"Dodo?" said a voice at her side, but she heard nothing, the silver plume still clutched to her chest, her body quaking, as she whispered, "*Wolfie, Wolfie . . .*"

"Dodo?"

The same voice again. Slowly, as if in a dream, hallucinating with fear and exhaustion, Dodo closed her eyes.

"Dorothy . . ."

Slower still, she turned from the lip of the shaft. It was as if she were a child, as if hearing in her sleep a parent's voice, thick with love, feeling the tender touch of a hand on her forehead.

She looked up and in the half-light she saw the father she'd not seen for six long years.

Pa. Pa. She was in his arms and he was holding her, her trembling subsiding in his warmth and strength.

After a few minutes, he pulled away to look at the daughter he'd not seen in so long, his eyes travelling over her face, his hands stroking her hair.

"Wolfie?" he whispered.

After a while he asked in a whisper, "Wolfie?" Dodo closed her eyes and gestured to the shaft.

"Oh God," he said. "Oh God."

Wordless, choking, eyes still closed, she raised the silver plume. Pa looked at the quivering strands, silver as moonlight in the glare of the headgear lamp.

"Hero," she said.

"Hero? . . . Here? How? . . . Oh God—So Wolfie went down . . ."

He pulled Dodo to his chest once more, rocking her and holding her.

Later, the wheels of the winding gear began to creak and they turned, as one, to the shaft.

A white glow spread across the sky. The crowd fell silent. The cage was winched to the surface, inch by hopeful inch, Seaton forgotten, the world forgotten, all eclipsed by the springing hope that was in the heart of every person there.

The roof of the cage crested the lip of the shaft. There was a gasping, a crying-out, a screaming, men, women, and children all surging forward.

In the white light of a new dawn stood Wolfie, a young man with thick chestnut hair, naked to the waist, his face and hands and chest black and grimy, one arm curled around the nose of a tall fine horse.

In a makeshift blindfold, the arms of Wolfie's jacket tied below his chin, his mane shorn, forelock shorn, stood Hero, arch and tall and quivering.

Behind them stood three wounded men, supported by rescuers. Three others lay on stretchers.

"Seven!" men were shouting. "Seven of 'em an' a 'orse!"

Hand grasped hand, eye met eye. Smiles and tears wreathed faces.

"Seven!" The word was passed from hand to hand,

to the back of the crowd. The sky brightened. The foreman called for men to go down, to explore the tunnels from this side, for more lights, more machinery, more men.

Soft, smiling rain fell. Wolfie untied the blindfold. The bar of the cage was lifted, and he led Hero out into a green and shining world.

Hero lifted his head. He snorted. Wolfie loosened his rope. Hero breathed, breathed again, nostrils wide, then he lifted his tail, he felt the clean wind on his cheeks and he cantered, kicking and snorting and bucking to the turf above the shaft. He lowered his muzzle to sniff at the grassy bank, at the wondrous green of it and he snorted and blew and pawed at it and struck at it to be sure, then doubled his knees, fell to the ground, and rolled and kicked and rolled and kicked and pawed the heavens with his four hoofs.

Hettie, waiting a little distance away with a bucket of fresh clean water, now watched as he slurped and sloshed, dipping his head almost to his cheekbones, and she rubbed at a patch of his neck till she saw, through her tears, the dappling of his coat.

Hettie, Dodo, and Pa were at Wolfie's side: They were holding him, hugging him, weeping, smiling, and shaking with tears and joy until Wolfie pulled away, pointing to Hero, saying, "Pa, Pa! Will you look at him?"

Hero lifted his head and trotted airily to the side

of the young man he loved. He pushed his head between Wolfie and Pa and nuzzled Wolfie. Wolfie's eyes were fierce and full, Pa's smiling and round with pride. Hero's head sank to the boy's naked shoulder and rested there.

AUTHOR'S NOTE

THE EXMOOR PONY

The Exmoor pony is the oldest and most primitive of Britain's native breeds. Early Celts used them to pull chariots, smugglers for moving contraband, and farmers for plowing, harrowing, shepherding, and pulling carts.

The First and Second World Wars had a devastating effect on them. By 1945 the breed was almost extinct, with only fifty registered mares and four stallions surviving nationwide. Incredibly, some were used for target practice by soldiers, many stolen for meat and sold in the cities of the North, and others taken to work the mines—often being smuggled out, transported by train, then sold at auction.

THE VICTORIA CROSS

The Victoria Cross is Great Britain's highest award for gallantry. Until the end of the First World War, holders of the Victoria Cross could be stripped of the honor for crimes such as desertion. In 1920 George V ruled that, once earned, a VC could never be taken away.

There are some (though not many) instances of holders of the VC being court-martialled.

The last great cavalry charge in British military history was at Cambrai, towards Moreuil Wood. For this, two officers were awarded VCs.

PIT PONIES

There are many instances of ponies being rescued from mines after disasters. In one case, three ponies lived for an incredible twenty-one days on rotten wood and water licked from the walls of the pit. These three ponies survived the West Stanley Pit disaster in 1909, in which 168 miners lost their lives.

On 25 November 1911, an explosion occurred in a North Staffordshire mine. On Monday, 18 December, a rescue party found three ponies alive six hundred yards from the shaft. Fifteen dead ponies were found.

Horses and ponies are referred to indiscriminately by miners as ponies. The taller animals tended to work nearer the shaft head or in drift mines.

THE MASSACRE AT WORMHOUT

The Norfolks and the Warwicks, ordered to defend Wormhout to keep the way clear for troops making their way back to Dunkirk, held up the enemy for an amazing twenty-four hours, allowing approximately

338,000 Allies to get to the beaches and await evacuation back to Britain.

On Monday, 27 May 1940, German planes dropped propaganda leaflets over Wormhout encouraging the British to surrender. The leaflets read: "Do you believe the stupid rumors that the Germans kill their prisoners? A decent enemy will be decently treated." The SS then committed an orgy of barbarism at Wormhout and the surrounding posts of Ledringhem and Esquelbecq. General Josef "Sepp" Dietrich commanded the SS *Leibstandarte* Division to massacre all prisoners. Wild with fury at the losses he'd incurred, trigger happy with drink, he unleashed a killing frenzy. The ground of the barn at Wormhout was a vision of hell, piled with half-naked bodies, their skulls smashed in, flesh mutilated, limbs twisted. British prisoners of war had been stripped naked to the waist, all identity tags removed, then shot at point-blank range. Dietrich bears the primary responsibility. Theoretically under the command of Himmler, in practice his special relationship with Hitler allowed him to disregard the chain of command. In return for his performance at Wormhout the Führer rewarded Dietrich with the order of the Iron Cross.

Most of the survivors said nothing to their families until the media gathered proof of the ordeal and their presence there. Those that did speak found that no one believed them until Otto Senf made his death-bed confession and the bodies were exhumed.

There is a monument on the road from Wormhout to Esquelbecq to the memory of the men of the Cheshires, Warwicks, and Royal Artillery who formed the rearguard action that played its part in the evacuation of a whole army.

On their courage depended the final outcome of the war.